Going Out with a Bang

"The thing is, the Idiots all have girlfriends, and that's because they have parties. I mean, when was the last time we had a party?"

"I've never had a party." Will looked downcast. I mean, there's no *way* his mum would let him. Wiping your shoes is one thing, but Will's mum makes *my* mum look like a party animal. If he behaves himself, he'll probably get some balloon animals and a magician when he's eighteen.

"Well." Dec smiled. "In three weeks, my mum and dad're going for a night away without me. You know what that means?"

"You're hoping they'll hire you a cute babysitter?" Will said, innocently. "Ow! You don't have to hit me."

"It *means*," Dec carried on, shaking his head, "we've got three weeks to organize the best party anyone at this school's ever been to. . ."

Sch

An almost-true story by Dylan Douglas (age 13)

Going Out with a Bang

Joel Snape

■SCHOLASTIC

Scholastic Children's Books,
Commonwealth House, 1–19 New Oxford Street,
London, WC1A 1NU, UK
a division of Scholastic Ltd
London ~ New York ~ Toronto ~ Sydney ~ Auckland
Mexico City ~ New Delhi ~ Hong Kong

First published in the UK by Scholastic Ltd, 2005

Copyright © Joel Snape, 2005
Cover illustration copyright © David Whittle, 2005

ISBN 0 439 97769 X

All rights reserved

Printed by Nørhaven Paperback A/S, Denmark

10 9 8 7 6 5 4 3 2 1

For my mum and dad, who are much nicer than anyone in this book

I was staring at the phone.

Come on, it seemed to be saying. *What's the matter with you? Scared?*

Hang on a minute.

Before I get into exactly why I was treating our phone as if it was a) alive and b) evil, there are a few things you probably need to know about me:

1. My name's Dylan.
2. I'm thirteen.
3. I'm never going to have any kind of facial piercing.
4. I can't dance, so don't even ask me.

And most importantly:

5. I don't have a mobile phone.

It's my mum's fault, really. My dad just thinks mobile phones are too expensive, which is the sort of thing I could probably get round with a bit of well-reasoned argument about how much money he spends on old records and stuff for his computer. My mum, on the other hand, thinks that mobile phones rot your brain, give off radioactive blasts and make you an easy target for muggers. Which is why, when I'm trying to organize my life, I have to use this clunky old beige thing with numbers for Lennon (my brother), Jess (my aunt) and Gran (my, um, gran) scribbled across a sticker on the front of it. Just picking up the receiver makes me feel about five times less cool than when I get to borrow someone's slimline polyphonic picture handset, or whatever. And tonight I actually thought it was taunting me.

It's Friday night, it seemed to be saying. *She's probably got something cool and exciting lined up – you know what she's like. In fact, she's probably gone out. Just put it off. Again. You big baby.*

"It's only seven o'clock," I mumbled to myself.

Whatever, said the phone. *What's the matter with you? Dec does this all the time. It's eeeasy. Chicken.*

"Fine," I said, grabbing the handset. That seemed to shut the phone up. I stared at the crumpled bit of paper with the number on it for the fiftieth time – just to make *really* sure that seven wasn't a one – and dialled. This wasn't so bad. Actually, it wasn't anywhere near as traumatic as I'd been expecting. Well, until somebody answered right in the middle of the first ring.

"Hello?" said a female voice.

"Karen!" I said, probably sounding a bit too relieved. "Hi, it's Dylan. Listen, I know we haven't spoken much at school, but I really like you and I think you're really clever and. . ." I glanced at the bit of paper I'd scribbled what I was going to say on. Yes, this was all going horribly wrong. Get on with it! ". . .I was wondering if you wanted to go to the cinema with me? Tomorrow night. Maybe."

"Well, that's very sweet and everything, but the problem is. . ." said the voice.

"I mean, it's OK if you're busy or if you don't want to or whatever, no problem, just asking."

This was probably too much backtracking. "But there's this great film on about, you know, this Maori girl who talks to whales, and I'd really like to see it but none of my mates want to, and I just thought that maybe you. . ."

"Um, actually?" said the voice, which – I suddenly realized – seemed to be on the verge of bursting out laughing. "This is Karen's mum."

Make that Coffee To Go. . .

If only I had a videophone, eh? On the other hand, that might have been even *more* embarrassing, because by the time I finally got to talk to Karen my face felt so red-hot that I was seriously worried about melting the handset. Even when I rang up my mate Dec for some post-humiliation damage control, it felt warm enough to make pancakes on. By the time I met up with him on Saturday morning, it had died down to a sort of low simmer, with my brain only going "Idiot!" every twenty minutes. Still, I didn't have too much trouble concentrating on what he was saying. . .

"You reckon girls can sense desperation," I said.

Dec nodded, sprinkling chocolate on his coffee and staring after a waitress as she walked past.

"Basically."

"And if you're too desperate, they won't fancy you," I carried on.

"Yep."

"But you can only get *less* desperate by getting a girlfriend."

"That's the problem." Dec looked pleased that I'd caught on so quickly. I would've shaken my head in disbelief – but that only encourages him.

Dec drives me mad. He is, admittedly, probably my best mate. He was, definitely, the only person I could safely tell about the way I'd messed up with Karen. And yes, all right, he was well ahead of me in the "coolness" stakes when we met, strolling into our first ever lesson at secondary school with his shirt untucked and tie off while I was sitting there freshly ironed and half-choking. None of which matters that much. No, what matters – according to Dec – is that I've never been out with a girl. In fact, not counting relatives, any playground game I played under the age of nine, and one unfortunate incident with Amanda Brown (don't ask), I've never even kissed one. Certainly not, you know, properly.

The *important* thing is, this tiny technicality, via some unwritten rule that only Dec understands, makes him the world authority on How To Impress Girls. The even more important thing is, he tends to do it in a totally inappropriate place – like, say, a coffee shop that you're only in because it's full of girls that you *don't* want overhearing you talking about that sort of thing. Bristol – that's where I live, incidentally – is *full* of places like that, little coffee shops or cafes or patisseries or whatever they're called. If you're the kind of person who likes pretending they're one of the cast of *Friends*, there're entire streets devoted to you. Pity I don't like coffee that much.

Anyway. The point is, we have conversations like this, in places like this, a *lot*. The usual procedure at this point is for me to roll my eyes, and Dec to ignore me and carry on.

I rolled my eyes and Dec carried on.

"It's like football. If you haven't scored for a while, your game's off and you can't concentrate properly. The important thing's to scrape together a result against anyone, even if it's a third-division side, and get your confidence back for the cup tie. Honestly."

He stopped for a slurp of moccachino, then said, "Basically, Dylan, if you ever want to have a chance with someone you fancy, it might be an idea just to try getting off with someone you don't."

A passing waitress scowled at us. Dec didn't even seem to notice.

"Anyway," he carried on, ripping off chunks of his blueberry muffin and shovelling them into his mouth. "What happened after you got Karen on the phone?"

"Well, she said I was sweet. . ."

"That's good," Dec mumbled.

"But she said she was busy tonight."

"That's bad."

"To be honest, I wasn't really thinking that straight," I said, thinking about how traumatized I'd been after realizing that I'd just asked out Karen's mum, "but I think maybe her mum said something before she handed the phone over. She sounded a bit . . . giggly."

"Hmm." Dec thought about it. "I dunno – Hannah said something about being busy tonight as well. Maybe they're having one of those slumber parties, or something."

"Yeah. . ." I sighed. "Hey, what're *you* up to this evening?"

"Um, I'm busy." Dec glanced at his watch. "Oops. That reminds me. Gotta go."

And Dec dashed off, stuffing the last of his muffin into his mouth and rushing for the door in a spray of crumbs.

Great. Now even my mates were standing me up.

You Are What You Eat

Woo! Exciting stuff so far, eh? Another weekend of doing nothing. Well, that's not strictly true, of course — on Saturday night I broke my all-time record for flicking toenail clippings into a bin — but apart from that, by Sunday morning I was starting to get a bit bored. And, obviously, the last thing I needed was my hippy sister questioning my taste in breakfast cereal. But, you know, she *always* does that.

"How can you *eat* that stuff?" asked Becky, giving me a look somewhere between "disapproving" and "horrified".

"I was just about to ask you the same thing," I mumbled, through a mouthful of sugar, marshmallows and the occasional flake of something-or-other.

"At least mine's good for me," Becky sniffed.

"So's mine." I shoved the packet towards her. "Look at that – thirty-three percent of my recommended daily allowance of riboflavin!"

"So what does riboflavin do?"

"Dunno." I grabbed another spoonful. "But another two bowls of this and I'll be *sorted*."

I think you can tell a lot about people by what they eat for breakfast. Take Becky – by the time I'd managed to stagger downstairs on this particular Sunday, she'd already munched her way through half a bowl of muesli (no sugar) with milk (soya), chopped up bananas (Fair Trade) and a glass of orange (organic). She's two years younger than my brother Lennon, four years older than me, and I'm *still* not sure how she turned out to be the hippy of the family. Ever seen a music festival on TV and noticed how hippies seem to dress in uniform? My sister looks *exactly* like that – clumpy boots, tatty combats, pierced nose – the T-shirt with a beardy revolutionary on it is optional. But even with all that she'd still be quite pretty if she didn't scowl all the time.

"Another two bowls of that and you'll be dead," she said, turning her nose up.

"I think I'd probably rather be dead than eat that health-mash, or birdseed, or whatever it's supposed to be."

One possibility, of course, is that Becky's overcompensating for the fact that she's jealous because she hasn't got a stupid flower-child name. I'm named Dylan, after – depending on what sort of mood my mum's in when you ask her – Bob Dylan (crusty guitarist from the 60s. . . .What can I say? My parents were still stuck in the 60s when they had me – thirty years later or whatever), Dylan Thomas (poet) or Dylan (the rabbit from *The Magic Roundabout*). I'm fairly sure only the first one's true, because my dad still plays Bob Dylan songs on the guitar occasionally, but you never can tell. My brother Lennon (typical breakfast – ideally a fry-up, realistically pretty much whatever's in his studenty flat when he gets up in the middle of the afternoon) is *definitely* named after the bloke from the Beatles who wrote "I Am The Walrus", because my mum used to have a crush on him. Lennon doesn't mind, because it's a good conversation starter and, well, because he never minds about anything, really. He's just too laid-back to get excited about stuff, which really annoys my sister (possibly because he's better at being "chilled" and hippyish than her) and my mum and dad (because he never seems to do any work).

Anyway, Becky isn't really named after anyone, possibly because neither my mum or dad like any musicians – or talking rabbits – with nice girls' names. She copes with the loss in her own way, mainly by doing parent-maddening things like putting her hair into dreadlocks, getting Henna tattoos, listening to crusty protest rock too loud and going out with someone with twenty-seven piercings. In fact, the only thing that occasionally lets her hippy image slip is that she's not shy about wasting the earth's precious natural resources when it suits her. Since she passed her driving test three months ago, she's abandoned her traditional horrified hippy outlook about how disgusting it is that people use their cars so much.

Which was why the next thing she said was:

"By the way, can I borrow the car today?"

My dad, who'd been ignoring our discussion about the merits of cereal – he's more of a tea and toast person – looked up from his paper.

"Hmm," he mumbled. "Going shopping?"

"Something like that."

"Isn't there some sort of protest thing going on in town today?" interrupted my mum, eyeing Becky suspiciously over her coffee.

"Oh, you mean the Reclaim the Streets thing." Becky looked the picture of innocence. "Yeah, I'd forgotten about that."

"Are you going?" My mum wasn't letting this go. Good for her.

"Well, I might drop by, if I'm in the area."

"Is Spider going?"

Spider. That's Becky's metal-studded boyfriend. Well, that's the only name he'll answer to. Honestly.

"I don't know," said Becky. She's a terrible liar, by the way. She sort of goes pink and tucks her chin in towards her chest whenever she's feeling guilty about something – that's why she'd never be able to get away with letting rabbits loose from a make-up testing lab. The police wouldn't need a lie detector – they'd just need to say, "Ladies and gentlemen of the jury, I put it to you that the defendant's suddenly started to look like a lobster."

"Shouldn't you be getting the bus?" I asked, as innocently as I could, "I mean, since it's a protest against cars and everything."

"Good point," agreed my dad, giving me a grin.

"I'm not sure I like you going to protests at your age," my mum joined in, taking up her usual position as the Responsible One. My mum's a teacher, so she has to be like that. "What if something happens?"

Becky just stared at us all taking sides against her evil polluting ways.

"*Fine.* I'll walk," she snarled, and stormed out of the room – we all stopped eating for long enough to hear her clump up the stairs and slam her bedroom door.

"That child," said my dad, shaking his head.

"It's just a phase," said my mum.

"I think you probably said that about Lennon, and look at him."

"I'm sure he's fine."

"I just hope he's doing some work," muttered my dad.

"You can ask him yourself," said my mum. My dad hardly ever talks much to Lennon on the phone. "He'll be coming down in a couple of weeks, remember."

Huh. Lennon's studying Political Something-or-Other at Birmingham University. At least, he says he's studying it. But anyway, it's not like he ever sticks around for long enough to talk about his course prospects. Everyone in my family knows that Lennon only ever comes home when he's a) sick of living on ready meals and doing his own washing or b) going drinking with his mates in Bristol. Weirdly, though, this was the first time I'd ever heard of him announcing his coming-home plans – he usually just turns up at midnight with a big grin on his face and a bag of dirty clothes. Still, I decided not to worry about it – it's always nice to have someone around who likes a bacon sandwich in the morning.

I Don't Like Mondays

The rest of Sunday seemed to fly by, although that's probably because I spent the entire morning watching TV, and most of the afternoon doing all my homework at the last minute, then worrying about the week coming up.

See, if there's one thing I disagree with Lennon about – apart from his awful taste in music – it's Mondays. He's the only person in the world who likes them . . . because he treats them like the start of a brilliant new week of lying in bed. Most other people don't like them much, but after all, the week has to start somewhere. But me? I *hate* Mondays.

For a start, there's the walk – my school's half an hour away from our house, because my mum was worried that I'd end up on drugs at the local school that most of my old friends went to. Anyway, *then* there's Admiral Ackbar – and if you've never done an hour's geography with someone who looks like an extra from *Star Wars* and gives out detentions for time-wasting, your Mondays are probably better than mine. *Then* there's German – nuff said – and *then* there's Matt the Idiot – I'll explain about him in a minute. But, even considering all that, this particular Monday was *especially* horrendous.

It all started at about five to nine. I was sitting next to Dec – I'd sort of hoped he might tell me what he'd got up to on Saturday evening, but he was doing some extremely last-minute maths homework, and it didn't seem fair to pester him. Apart from that, I was trying to look inconspicuous – I wasn't exactly looking forward to seeing Karen, especially if she'd told her mates about my mum-charming phone skills. Although, as it turned out, I probably didn't need to worry.

"Hi guys!" said Hannah, clattering through the door and dashing over to her table in one, excited-looking move.

As far as our school goes, Hannah's part of the "in" crowd – which means that she's officially the closest we get to one of those girls that get paid for going to parties and having their photos taken. If there were GCSEs in Being Popular, she'd be taking them three years early.

"Hi!" said about half a dozen girls.

"Hi-ee!" Rachel was next in, waving like she was on the red carpet at the Oscars instead of strolling into her classroom on a rainy Monday.

"Hi-eee!" said the girls again.

"Hey!" Karen – yes, *that* Karen – was the last of the It girls to turn up. And she didn't even look at me.

"Hi-eeee!" said the rest of the girls. A couple of them even giggled.

This was weird. On Monday morning, everyone's supposed to just sit around staring into space, knowing that they've got a whole week of maths, assemblies, weaving inventions from the nineteenth century and Admiral Ackbar ahead of them. People chat about their weekends, and that's fine, but no one's supposed to seem *happy* that they're at school – well, apart from Scott "The Swot" Forrester. But this morning, people were whispering, sniggering and generally looking as if they were enjoying being here. This was *really* weird.

"What's going on?" I said to Dec.

"No idea." Dec looked as confused as I was. "Hey, Hannah. . ."

"Heyyyy!" said the next person into the classroom. The next, huge, blond-haired rugby-playing person.

"Hi, Matt!" chorused the It girls.

"Oh, great," said Dec. "The Idiots have landed."

To be fair, Matt hasn't always been an Idiot. In fact, I was actually, well, *friends* with him back in primary school. My mum used to love him – she still thinks of him as "that nice polite boy" who I don't see any more. I think the point when we started to "grow apart" (the parental translation for "hate each other") was when Matt abandoned traditional breaktime sports like Throw The Tennis Ball At Each Other As Hard As You Can and started playing rugby. And getting in fights. And not even the brilliant "Push him over! Rip his shirt a bit!" fights that're actually pretty good fun when you're nine, but proper, pick-on-someone-smaller-than-you-and-kick-them-when-they're-down fights. And it didn't help when he started hanging around with Keith Sharp (who, I swear, just has one huge eyebrow) and Nick Bishop (looks like a weasel).

"What's he so cheerful about?" I said, watching Matt high-five his fellow Idiots and grin at the girls.

"Dunno," said Dec. "But if I had to guess, I'd say he's just got back together with—"

"What's up, dudes?" Will interrupted, slamming his bag down on the table between us.

I've been friends with Will even longer than Dec – he's practically the only other person in my class who went to school with me and Matt. The thing is, while Matt was turning into an Idiot, Will stayed exactly the same. He's still interested in the same sort of stuff we were into when we were ten, although he pretends that they're more grown-up now. "Toys" aren't toys, because they're "collectibles", kids' cartoons have turned into anime films full of people getting their heads chopped off by demons, and he plays computer games full of psycho gangsters instead of ones where a loveable tiger smashes crates and collects gold coins. His hair's exactly the same mess it always was – this huge light-brown mop that makes him look like a mad professor in training. And – this sort of goes without saying – he really isn't that bothered about what girls think of him.

Matt can't stand him – which is one of the reasons we "grew apart" – but Will gets on OK-ish with Dec. Still, I sometimes get the feeling that they're just putting up with each other for my sake – like when we're in town, and Dec's complaining that the comic shop smells of fat people. Well, that's what happened until Dec got banned from the comic shop.

"Good weekend?" I asked.

"Yeah, brilliant!" said Will, still messing about with his bag. "Watched the wrestling on Saturday, and then there were four hours of *Simpsons* episodes on Sunday."

"Oh, that explains why everyone else is so happy," Dec joined in, with just a bit of a smirk. "They're probably just pleased about The Rock winning the championship."

"Yeah, but everyone already knew he was going to," Will pointed out. "It's all fake, remember?"

"Shut up, Will." Dec elbowed him.

From there, we somehow got into an argument about why wrestling's better than football (basically, nobody gets hit with a ladder when they're playing football), and after Chris and Scott (mad-keen footballers from the table next to us) joined in, we couldn't talk about anything else until the bell rang. It looked as if the mystery of the happy people was going to have to wait until later. . . .

Playing the Field

Unfortunately, by breaktime we weren't any closer to working out what was going on. I'd already suffered through an entire hour of quadratic equations, which didn't give my brain much chance to worry about anything else. I was off in my own little world when Will nudged me.

"Eurgh. They're doing it again." He was staring at the field in what I suppose you'd call horrified fascination. We were sitting around on the grim metal benches close to the school building, but Will was craning around to look at the cluster of people in the middle of the football pitch. Will *hates* football.

"Doing what?" I said, turning round to see what he was looking at. "Oh. Eurgh."

Matt and Rachel were kissing – leech-style – in probably the last place you'd pick if you were trying to be inconspicuous. They were surrounded by the other Idiots – as well as most of the It girls. Unbelievable.

"Don't encourage them," I said, giving Will a shove.

"What are you on about?"

Will was still just staring at them. He might not be that interested in girls, but he's got a sort of scientific curiosity about what other lads get up to.

"Look at that." Dec sauntered up with his hands in his pockets. "True love. Isn't it marvellous?"

"Bleuch," said Will.

The weird thing about the Idiots is, they make asking girls out seem really easy. You pester girls, you get knocked back, you pester some more girls, then maybe you eventually get a snog. Then you dump the girl that snogged you and go after another one. I've got this bit of my brain that goes into red-alert embarrassment mode if I even *talk* to a girl I like – but Matt doesn't seem to have one. I actually think maybe he's wrecked it by nutting people on the rugby pitch. As far as I can tell, he's been "going out" with Rachel about five times in the past six months. Then he dumps her for a couple of weeks and she cries until her mascara's a splodgy mess – then he asks her out again, and everything's lovely. Aaaand repeat. You'd think she'd be able to see the pattern by now.

"Why does she put up with him?" I wondered out loud.

"Because she's daft," said Dec, not looking anywhere near as decisive as he sounded. "But when did they get back together?"

I shrugged. And then, suddenly, Hannah was right next to us.

"What happened to you on Saturday, Dec?" she said, doing her usual fake-ditzy hair-playing thing. I know she's doing it on purpose and it really annoys me – but I still can't help fancying her. Dec gave her a puzzled look.

"Nothing much. Why, what should I have been doing?"

Now it was Hannah's turn to look puzzled. "Matt's party. Everyone else was there. Didn't he invite you?"

"*Ohhh*," said Dec, recovering fast. "Matt's *party*. Yeah, of *course* he invited me – I was just a bit busy. Was it any good?"

"Yeah, brilliant! You should *definitely* come to the next one."

"Okaaayy," started Dec, but Hannah was already scanning the field.

"Oh, isn't that *sweet!*" she exclaimed, spotting Matt and Rachel. Then she started waving at another couple walking in the general direction of Matt's gang. "Hey! Guys!"

And she was off again.

"I don't believe it!" Dec was fuming. "He didn't invite us! He probably did it on purpose! Well, I *do* believe it, because he's an idiot, but. . ."

"Who cares?" I heard Will say. Another major difference between the two of them's that Will just can't understand why you'd want to go to a party being thrown by somebody you don't like. And Dec can't understand why you wouldn't. It drives them both mad.

"Dylan? You used to be friends with Matt, didn't you? Why didn't he ask you?" Dec was demanding, but I wasn't really listening. I was too busy watching the two people that Hannah was catching up with.

It was Karen. And Keith Sharp. Holding hands.

Karen. Busy. Saturday night. Aaaaaargh.

Oh, and here's the other problem with Mondays – I was about to get even *closer* to Matt. . .

The thing is, ignoring Matt's hard enough when there's a field between you and him – when he's talking directly into your ear, it's pretty much impossible.

"So there I was. . ." he was whispering at me. I *was* trying to ignore him, but I wasn't having much luck. "Dancing with Hannah. . ." I stared extra-hard at my book, hoping that Matt would notice how interested I was in the picture of two people ordering a ticket in the *Bahnhof* and shut up for a minute. . . Nope. "And, you know, I just thought, well, since we're this close. . ."

"Matthew! *Was essen Sie zum frühstück?*"

Genius. I wish I could say I'd thought of throwing a surreal spanner into the conversation by barking questions at Matt in German, but that was Miss Spencer. Up until she arrived at the start of the year, I thought I was going to get through my entire school life without ever fancying a teacher. Every other member of staff either has facial hair (most of the men, Mrs Twigger), looks like Admiral Ackbar from *Star Wars* (Miss

Bickham – and honestly, the glasses don't help) or has about three years to go until they start their pension. When Miss Spencer turned up, looking like Natalie Portman, with dark hair and tight jeans, she didn't have much competition. The only problem is, she seems sort of determined to stop everyone fancying her by being really unpopular. Apart from being the strictest teacher I've ever had, she started the term off with the genius idea of randomly choosing who we'd sit next to for the rest of the year. Dec, who I usually sit with whenever I get the chance, fluked a seat on the back row with Hannah. I got . . . Matt.

It isn't so bad, though, because she leans over your desk when she's annoyed with you. And she leans over our desk a *lot*, because she doesn't appreciate people talking during her lessons.

"Um. . . *Ich spiele fussball?*" tried Matt. Somewhere at the back, I heard Dec snigger.

Well, to be fair, it was a nice try – he might even have got away with it, if Miss Spencer hadn't been asking him what he eats for breakfast. And no, Matt isn't one of those people who eats, sleeps and breathes football – he spends all his spare time a) trying to grope girls, b) showing off about how many girls he's groped and c) playing rugby. It obviously doesn't leave him much time for things like "Learning German", because *fussball*'s just about the only word he knows. Miss Spencer gave him a stare and carried on with the lesson. Matt went back to ignoring her and whispering at me.

"So . . . I've got my hand up the back of her shirt, and. . ." I thought about pushing him off his chair, then decided it wasn't worth the bother. "She wears a bra! I mean, I can't believe that. A bra! She looks like an ironing board. I mean. . ."

"Matt," I said, trying to sound bored instead of jealous. "I'm really not that both—"

"Dylan! Have you got something to say to the rest of the class?" OK, so it wasn't a full-on lean – but Miss Spencer was definitely giving me one of her angriest looks. I tried to do a "who, me?" expression.

"I wasn't. . ."

"*Have* you?"

"It's not. . ."

"HAVE you?"

"No, miss."

"Right. Not another word from either of you." Keith muttered, "Naughty, naughty," from somewhere at the back, and there were a few sniggers.

Matt nudged me and whispered, being really quiet this time.

"I'd probably have invited you, but you've got to ditch that nerd you hang around with."

I spent the rest of the lesson biting my tongue out of rage. I was so annoyed that I even forgot to feel sorry for Miss Spencer when she did her usual plea for people to think about going on the annual German exchange and got a roomful of blank stares. In fact, I was all set to have a good moan at Dec and (hopefully) make myself feel better as soon as the bell rang, but he grabbed me first.

"Will's house," he said. "After school. I've got a plan."

"I've had enough of it," said Dec, slamming his fist down on the desk for extra drama. A model of Jango Fett fell on the floor.

"Had enough of what?" said Will, munching a biscuit and giving Jango his blaster back.

Going from the rest of Will's house into his room's sort of like stepping from a Werther's Original ad straight into a high-tech Land Of

The Giants. Everything else in the house is . . . nice. There's no other word for it. Nice sofa, nice wallpaper, nice little pictures as you go up the stairs, nice lampshades, nice everything. That's until you get to Will's room, which is, um, insane. Every shelf's rammed full of toys, all arranged into little scenes: Mace Windu fighting Count Dooku on top of his stereo, Batman and Spawn at either end of his bookshelf, a TIE Fighter dangling from the ceiling. It's taken him years to make it look like that – you get the impression his mum's just given up on it and concentrated on filling the rest of the house with little porcelain statues of dogs. I mean, she's a nice enough *person* – as long as you wipe your feet – but I try to avoid going round to Will's house, because she doesn't seem to approve of me or Dec very much.

When Dec decided that he needed to talk to us, though, it seemed like the safest house to meet at. Mainly because Will's mum wasn't in.

"I don't have a girlfriend – well, not at the moment, anyway," announced Dec. "Dylan, you've never had a girlfriend." He paused and glanced around. "And Will's probably never going to get a girlfriend."

"Hey!" protested Will.

"Shut up, Will." Dec didn't even miss a beat. "The thing is, the Idiots all have girlfriends, and that's because they have parties. I mean, when was the last time we had a party?"

"I've never had a party." Will looked downcast. I mean, there's no *way* his mum would let him. Wiping your shoes is one thing, but Will's mum makes *my* mum look like a party animal. If he behaves himself, he'll probably get some balloon animals and a magician when he's eighteen.

"Well." Dec smiled. "In three weeks, my mum and dad're going for a night away without me. You know what that means?"

"You're hoping they'll hire you a cute babysitter?" Will said, innocently. "Ow! You don't have to *hit* me."

"It *means*," Dec carried on, shaking his head, "we've got three weeks to organize the best party anyone at this school's ever been to. I mean, seriously – something that everyone's going to talk about for ages. Something really special."

"Like what?" I asked, worrying about what "special" might mean. For all I knew, Dec might be picturing fire-eaters or acrobats or something.

"Well, we'll have to think about that," Dec admitted. "But it's got to be better than anything Matt's done. And we'll, I don't know, print proper invitations. It'll be great."

"Is that OK with your mum and dad?" Will looked in awe of such cool parents.

"Pffft." Dec did a dismissive little wave. "They don't have to know about it. Anyway, anyone can come, except for the Idiots. And. . ." He stared at Will. "We all have to invite a girl."

"Who?" said Will, looking slightly frightened at the idea.

"Anyone," said Dec.

"What if whoever it is says no?"

"Then ask someone else." Dec was getting frustrated. "But this is our big chance, so everyone has to make *sure* someone comes. No excuses."

"I dunno *who* I'm going to ask. . ." Will mumbled.

"Same here," I said. "It took me about a year to get round to asking Karen out, and she decided to go for Keith the Idiot instead."

"You'll find someone." Dec grinned at me. "Anyway, that's the point – you've only got three weeks and you *have* to ask someone – it'll be good practice."

34

"Who're *you* going to ask?" I stared at Dec.

"Oh, I've got an idea about that as well." Dec grinned even wider. "I'll let you know if I need any help."

By the time I got home, I was actually pretty excited. I'd had plenty of time to get worked up about the idea of a party – and, come on, three weeks was far enough away not to worry about finding a date, wasn't it? Well, probably, anyway. The only problem, I thought, was Dec's "something special" idea, and I was sure we'd be able to manage that. In fact, I had some pretty good ideas about where to start. Unfortunately, when I tried putting them into practice, everything started to go horribly wrong.

"Hey, Mister Tambourine Man – what's up?"

Two things you need to know about my brother Lennon:

1) He's the only person who *ever* calls me that. It's a Bob Dylan thing. My parents' favourite crusty wrote this song called "Mr Tambourine Man", and my brother thinks it's funny and, well, let's just say the novelty wore off at about the time he bought me a tambourine one Christmas.

2) He never does any work. Not as far as I can

tell, anyway. As I mentioned, he's supposed to be doing Political Something-or-Other, but I've never seen him bring any books home or worry about an essay.

It was about five o'clock when I rang him, so I thought he'd probably just be finishing a hard day in the library. He was in the pub.

I explained the situation, although it didn't help that I could hear people hooting in the background at the other end of the line. Lennon thought for a second, and shouted:

"Elephants."

"Elephants?" For a second, I thought maybe he was talking to someone in the pub. Although that wouldn't have made much sense either, come to think of it.

"I've always thought I'd like to go to a party with elephants. Or maybe camels. Trained ones."

"I'm not a James Bond villain," I reminded my space-case brother. "I'm on a bit of a budget, in fact."

"Oh!" said Lennon. "Um . . . tequila roulette?"

"I'm thirteen," I pointed out.

"Right, right. . ." Lennon yawned. "Good point. Maybe you should get a clown."

"I'm going to hang up the phone now."

"Good idea," said Lennon, sounding like he was already drifting off.

I hung up. Plan B it was, then.

Unfortunately for plan B, the internet wasn't much use either. OK, so let's face it: the internet's brilliant for clips of people crashing their BMXs, or stick men doing kung fu, or pictures of Lara Croft with her top off, or other stuff that sends my e-mail into "Forget getting any more messages, EVER" mode. But for useful stuff, like how to throw a party when you haven't got any money? Hopeless. There were plenty of sites offering stag and hen nights, a few devoted to throwing the best possible party for your spoilt seven year old, but absolutely nothing for teenagers. I clicked on my e-mail in frustration, which brought up an e-mail from my crazy German penfriend, which just read:

Hello Dylan!
How are you? I hope the winter is not too cold in England. Last week I am going skiing – I think that you cannot ski in England, even though it is cold. My dog is sick at the moment, but the veterinarian said that it was not serious.

Write to me soon!
Tchuss
Rudi

Look – he's *insane*. That's why I'm not going on the German exchange. I mean, where'd he get "veterinarian" from? And "I think you cannot ski"? What's the point in even replying to that? I thumped out a quick e-mail back – in English – then cut 'n' pasted it into freetranslation.com. Voila! Perfectly decent German letter. Of course, the grammar might be a bit shabby, but I'm sure Rudi can work it out – after all, I have to deal with his complete inability to grasp the past tense. I gave it a quick read through – nope, didn't understand any of it – and hit Send.

I'm completely aware that some people might regard this as cheating – I'd call it "efficiency" or "using all the means at my disposal". After all, it's a good use of my computer skills.

From: qui_gon_jinn6@hotmail.com
To: dylan25@hotmail.com
Dude,
Check this out!
;c) Laterz
Will

And suddenly, my screen was covered in cats in hats, dancing to a rock song. As I said – technology is brilliant. OK, so I'm not too keen on the fact that Will's named himself after a *Star Wars* character – or that he's the sixth person to do it – but dancing kittens are great.

I was still humming their crazy kitten tune as I strolled down the stairs and into the living room.

"Were you talking to Lennon on the phone?" said my mum, lowering whatever book she was reading about the oppression in, well, wherever.

"Erm, yeah. Why?"

I'll say it again – this is the problem with having a great big clunky land-line phone just within hearing range of the living room.

"Did you ring him?"

"Yeah."

"Why?" Good question, I suppose. It's not like I'm in the habit of calling Lennon up for a chat about politics. Still, didn't she trust me?

"Oh, just for a chat, you know. I've been . . . missing him recently."

I don't know why I even bothered lying. And I definitely don't know why I said something that stupid. Still, my mum didn't seem to notice.

"Tch." She did her teacher-y glower of

disapproval. "You should have told me. I wanted to talk to him."

"Yeah, but he was in a rush."

"Well, I hope he rings us back fairly soon." My mum shook her head. "He's *so* difficult to get hold of, and I really ought to talk to him about the wedding."

Blaaargh. *That* was why Lennon was coming home. I'd forgotten about the wedding.

The Happiest Day of your Life?

"I don't see what's so bad about a wedding," said Will.

I groaned, and skidded off-piste into a tree.

Well, no, not literally, of course. What with homework and everything, it's pretty tough to go snowboarding on a Tuesday night, so we occasionally have to make do with going round to each other's houses to play PS2 games. Dec's house is best, because he's got the biggest TV – but Dec had disappeared without a word straight after school. Mine's second best, because even though you have to play on a tiny portable, nobody tuts at you when you shout at the screen.

I hit Restart and turned to Will.

"You don't know my aunt Jess."

It was my own fault. I'd known about the

wedding for ages – the invitations arrived *months* ago, all gold handwriting on creamy-pink bits of card, but I'd sort of managed to put it to the back of my mind. I think even my mum'd tried to forget it – there's something about my aunt Jess that makes my mum look almost disorganized. From the moment my cousin Marie announced she was tying the knot with an accountant (ugh) called Paul, my mum had been getting phone calls about table settings, food, who didn't like who and what a hassle it all was. As the day approached, though, all the fuss had died down a bit, and I'd managed to forget that I was going to get crowbarred into a suit and tie and forced to tell all my old relatives that, no, I still wasn't "courting" with anyone.

"Hey!" said Will, suddenly brightening up as he dived through a 20,000 point snowflake. "Maybe you'll meet someone to go to the party with!"

"Doubt it." I shook my head, thinking about the idea of trying to chat up girls in front of my family. "I mean, half the people there're related to me, and the other half . . . well, I dunno."

"Hmm." Will nodded.

"Anyway, what about you?" I said. "I mean, I'm

not taking the mick or anything, but your mum hardly ever lets you leave the house – how're you going to ask someone if you don't talk to the girls at school?"

"Oh, I don't know," said Will. "There're other ways to meet girls, y'know."

One other thing about Will – he can't wink. I mean, Dec and me have both tried to teach him, but he looks like he's just been hit in the eye by a wasp, or something, whenever he tries. But just as I grabbed the joypad back off him, it looked as if he was trying to. . .

When I sat down in Wednesday's German lesson, I was – well, a bit distracted. I mean, for a start, I thought I was in for the usual combo of boredom and annoying Idiot-speak. For another, I was still wondering about my mates – about Will's cryptic comment and the way Dec kept disappearing. And I couldn't stop worrying about the wedding and our non-existent plans for the party.

So anyway, put all that together, and you've got a fair idea of why I didn't notice Kate. Well, not straight away. OK, so obviously, I noticed someone was sitting at the desk in front of me, where no one's sat since the incident with Matt's lighter, but in my midweek gotta-get-through-this haze, I just thought, *Hmm, someone's changed seats – Miss Spencer isn't going to be happy about that.*

Miss Spencer's first announcement didn't do anything for my excitement levels – she was still looking for people interested in going on her exchange trip to Germany. (Current sign-up rate: still zero from our class. Will told me Scott Forrester signed up on about the first day they announced the exchange, but I didn't think they'd let him go on his own.)

"Look," she tried. "Don't *any* of you want to meet your penfriends?"

As if – my penfriend was crazy enough on e-mail. I hated to think what he'd be like in person.

Of course, Matt's response wasn't quite that well thought-out. Well, what do you expect? He's an Idiot.

"Two world wars and one world cup, doo-dah, doo-dah!"

"Matthew!"

So it was only when Miss Spencer finished calling him a Neanderthal that things got interesting.

". . .Everyone should at least *think* about it.

After they've come here, you get the chance to go to Heidelberg. It's a lovely city, and it'll be an invaluable experience for *most* of you." Miss Spencer gave Matt a pointed stare. "Oh, and I nearly forgot – we have a new student. *Klasse*, this is Kate."

"Hi, everyone," said Kate, turning around and giving the class a little wave and a big smile.

My eyes nearly popped out of my head.

Sorry if that sounds weird. I didn't just fancy Kate because *anybody* would. I mean, she was really pretty, but she doesn't have lips like Salma Hayek's or a nose like Heather Graham's or a bum as nice as Kylie's. She has nice hair (brownish), nice eyes (blueish) and a bit of a tan. But when she smiled, suddenly she was the most gorgeous girl I'd ever seen.

Don't get me wrong – it wasn't love at first sight. I don't even believe in love at first sight, to be honest. The whole idea seems a bit weird and stalker-ish, especially if the feeling isn't mutual. So no, it wasn't that. But I really, *really* fancied her. I was still trying to work out the best way of looking cool in a German lesson if you're not very good at German, when Matt nudged me in the arm and gave me one of his smirks.

"Well, I would."

Aaargh.

I don't think I learned much German in that lesson.

Firstly, there were the images that kept popping, unannounced, directly into my brain: Matt snogging Kate on the football field; Matt dancing with Kate at a party; Matt and Kate getting married, and so on.

Secondly, there was Kate: as well as having the nicest smile in the world, it turned out that she was clever (she actually knew the German for "I want to be an investigative journalist") and funny (she did an impression of Uter, the chubby exchange student from *The Simpsons*, going "Don't rush me! I'm full of chocolate!"). She was *brilliant*.

Anyway, I'm not sure how I got away with it – Miss Spencer's usually watching like a hawk for people who aren't paying attention, and I was quite clearly just staring at the back of Kate's head. I was still sitting there, shell-shocked, fifty minutes later, when Dec leaned over my desk on his way out.

"Meet me outside the gates at home time. Don't bring Will."

It's Great When You Skate

"I'm not doing it," I said, in my firmest You're-Just-Wasting-Your-Time voice.

"I'm not really asking you to *do* anything, if you don't want to," pointed out Dec.

"I don't want to, and I'm not going to."

"Just come with me."

"No, because I know what's going to happen," I said, stubbornly.

After German, my mind was racing with ways to a) talk to Kate after school, b) appear much cooler/funnier/more attractive than I actually am and c) keep her away from Matt the Idiot. But then it occurred to me – there was no way I was going to do that tonight, after her first day at school. And however persistent Matt the Idiot was, it was unlikely that he was going to get to twang her bra straps, or whatever, that particular evening.

Besides, I didn't *really* know what was going to happen, whatever I told Dec. If I had, I'd definitely have walked off then and there, and not even given him a chance to talk me round. As it was, if we kept walking in the direction of the skatepark, it was only a matter of time.

Bristol skatepark's great. They might not give enough money to schools (according to my mum) or be any good at collecting bins (Dad), but there's one thing I'll say for our council – they know how to build a skatepark. A couple of years ago, they decided that something to keep The Kids out of trouble might be a good idea – and at that point they must have got some lottery money or something, because instead of just sticking a half-pipe in a children's playground, they built this enormous skate-wonderland full of grind rails, vert ramps and funboxes. On Saturdays you can sit there for ages, just watching people pull cool tricks or (even better) slam into things.

It didn't really stop the trouble, of course. The kids who used to skive off school, smoke, drink cider, spraypaint stuff and threaten other kids, didn't stop. Now they all just do it in one place, which is why all the half-pipes are covered in graffiti, the paths are all covered in crisp packets and the grass verges around the park are covered in nutters. That's why the skatepark's fine on a weekend, when there are parents around to watch their kids work on kickflips, but not exactly the greatest place to go after school. None of this matters to Dec, though. He goes there all the time – and he had a plan.

The thing is, though: I can't even skateboard. I had a go once, when I was nine, except that I'd forgotten the golden rule of any sport – if you've never tried it on flat land, *don't try it on the steepest hill in your town*. One pair of ripped trousers and two severely scraped elbows later, and that was it for me and skateboarding.

Dec's much more sensible. He can ollie things, do 50–50 grinds and manage decent manual rolls – hey, I can play Tony Hawk – they're all things he learned to do before skating was *quite* as cool as it is now. And that's enough for him. Ten minutes of serious skating and he's off wandering around and chatting to all the thrasher girls who sit on the grass banks. Which is where I was supposed to come in.

The reason he'd had to dash off on Saturday, Dec explained, was that he'd met a girl on one of his earlier trips to the park. She was really pretty, he thought he was in with a chance, and she had this mate who sort of wouldn't give them any time to themselves, and . . . and it was about that point that I worked out what was going on.

This wasn't Dec setting me up, whatever he said – it was Dec trying to get rid of someone else. And the weird thing about Dec is, he thinks you won't notice when he tries this stuff.

"Look, all you have to do is talk to Natalie's mate for a bit while we go for a walk somewhere. Otherwise I'll never get rid of her."

"Is Natalie's mate pretty?"

"Yeah! Fairly."

"What do you mean, 'fairly'?"

"I think you'll like her."

"Do *you* like her?"

"Not as much as I like Natalie."

Suddenly, I remembered our conversation in the cafe.

"Is she third division?"

"Ha! I'd say she's. . ." Dec gave it a bit of thought. "First division. Just not premier league. It's an easy away win."

"Why didn't you ask Will?"

"Because he's already been relegated."

That carried on right until we were at the skatepark. Worried as I was, I had to admit that I wanted to meet Dec's potential girlfriend – and I couldn't help wondering what her mate would be like. I probably wasn't going to fancy her as much as Kate, or anything, but there was no harm in looking, was there?

"There they are," said Dec, as we walked towards the gates.

Dec pointed at two girls lying together on one of the grass banks. They were both wearing identical black hooded tops and combats, although one of them had brown hair and the other one was blonde. I couldn't really tell what they looked like at that distance – and besides, I didn't know which one was which.

"Come on."

Before I knew it, Dec had taken his school shirt off and stuffed it in his bag. Underneath, he was wearing a T-shirt with some sort of ultra-trendy kung-fu monkey logo on. What with that, his black school trousers and his jacket, he didn't look much different to most of the people skating. And I was still wearing my school uniform.

I couldn't believe it. He'd probably been plotting this ever since that little chat in the coffee shop.

"Oh, this is great. Thanks for warning me," I said.

"It'll be fine. Come on."

"Hang on a. . . No, just stop right. . . Oh, I don't believe this." I tried to protest, but Dec was already heading straight for them.

Up closer, I started to feel even worse. Both girls were plastered with black mascara, but the blonde one was really pretty – and she was obviously Dec's type. The other one wasn't ugly, exactly, but she was really pale, had a weird smile and . . . well, she looked mad. I don't know what it was – maybe the stupid pink hair extensions, maybe the tatty, fingerless gloves or clump boots – but she just had this aura that said, Danger: Keep Away. They were both giggling at nothing in particular, except that the dangerous-looking one was making a sort of snorting noise while she did it. Eep.

"Natalie, Fiona – this is Dylan," said Dec, stepping forward with his best girl-charming smile firmly in place. Natalie, I figured out, was the blonde one, who smiled at Dec. Fiona was the crazy-looking one, who just scrunched up her nose a bit.

They stopped laughing and sat up to give me deliberately serious looks.

"Pleased to meet you."

"Nice tie."

And both of them exploded into giggles again. I suppose I could have at least taken the tie off.

From there, everything went pretty much as you'd expect it to, especially if you've ever been set up by a mate who's using you as back-up. Dec and Natalie flirted and laughed and found excuses to touch each other – me and Fiona sat with our arms folded and about a metre of space between us. I couldn't even think of anything to talk about – I hated the band on the T-shirt she was wearing, she probably hated people who wore school uniform. Or, in fact, bothered with going to school. After what felt like three hours of painful silence (about ten minutes), I stood up and cleared my throat.

"I've, erm, got to go. I've got stuff to do."

Dec sat up – he'd been practically nose-to-nose with Natalie, and he didn't look happy about the interruption. His "date" was going a lot better than mine.

"Like what?"

"Erm . . . homework," I said, not thinking it through. Again. "I've got that essay to do for Admiral Ackbar."

Fiona gave me a look that said I'd just plummeted another ten points on her ever-likely-to-fancy scale. Homework? Clearly not a big priority for her. Dec didn't seem that bothered, either.

"Oh, just leave it. She never gives anyone detentions for not handing stuff in. Just tell her your sister recycled it, or something."

"Yeah, but I've got other stuff to do as well. Wedding stuff, you know. . ."

"You're getting *married*?" Natalie said, in pretend outrage. Nope, I didn't think that had helped my chances either.

"Fair enough," said Dec, giving me an I'm-not-coming-with-you wave.

"Anyway, I'll just be . . . erm. . ." I trailed off. Somehow, Dec's face was back within about three millimetres of Natalie's. "Right, so I'll be. . . Right." I looked away. I really didn't need to see *that*.

I walked off with my hands stuffed into my pockets, trying to do that casual stroll that you can only really pull off if you've got trousers like a tent. There's a definite trick to having a cool walk – it's all about looking as if you're in no particular hurry to get anywhere, as if you're too busy thinking deep thoughts to worry too much about where you're going or what's happening around you. I think I was managing quite well – at least, right until I heard a yell and a sixteen-year-old skater slammed into me.

Hope for the Best,
Plan for the Wurst

I had plenty of time to think on my way home. To be fair, I spent the first ten minutes worrying about whether the gash in my elbow was ever going to stop bleeding and trying not to get blood on my shirt. Then I spent another twenty minutes fuming and thinking about elaborate ways to get my revenge on Dec. Luckily – well, sort of – the skatepark's about an hour's walk from my house, so I started to think about slightly more constructive things – like what our "something special" for the party was going to be, and who I could ask. I wasn't having much luck with either, especially considering that most girls I went near seemed to end up giggling hysterically. Still, I should have known better than to do what I did when I got home. I mean, I hadn't lost *that* much blood.

"Mum. . ." I said, wandering into the living room. "What're you supposed to do at parties?"

"I think you're a bit old for birthday parties now, love." My mum didn't look up from the books she was marking. I tried again.

"Not for my birthday, that's not for ages. It's going to be at Dec's house."

"Really?" She frowned and scribbled something on someone's work. "Have you got him a present?"

"It's not a birthday party, Mum," I said. "It's just . . . a party. You know, Pringles instead of pineapple on sticks, that sort of thing. I don't even think we're going to bother playing pass the parcel."

"Who's organizing it?"

"Well, me, Dec and Will. But I haven't got any ideas, so, you know. . ."

"What happened to your elbow?"

Honestly, my mum'd be a great police interrogator. The way she changes the subject, you haven't even got chance to think up a convincing lie.

"I got hit by a skateboarder."

"A skateboarder *punched* you?"

"No, he sort of crashed into me. Look. . ."

"What does Dec's mum think?"

"About the skateboarder? She doesn't know, it only just happened." My mum gave me a frown, and I realized she'd gone back to talking about the party. See what I mean about changing the subject? "I'm not sure Dec's told her. . ." I realized I'd made a massive tactical error as soon as I said that, and backpedalled furiously. "But, you know, I'm sure she's fine with it. It's not a big thing."

"Well, just make sure you ask her." My mum did a quick series of ticks. "I think maybe you're a bit young for that sort of party."

"Lennon used to go to them all the time," I pointed out. "He even had one here."

Obviously, as soon as I said this, I remembered a) exactly what had happened and b) that this was another huge mistake. My mum finally looked up.

"That's exactly what I'm talking about. Do you have *any* idea how much trouble it is to get guacamole off a ceiling?"

"Look, everyone has them," I tried, still back-pedalling. "Matt had one on Saturday. I didn't get invited, of course."

"That's probably because you never invite him round here any more. How *is* Matt these days? I saw his mum at the supermarket the other day."

Honestly. My mum's got no idea. She carried on, apparently not noticing that I was practically gasping with disbelief.

"She was saying he's captain of the rugby team this year. Maybe you should get more involved in team sports."

Hnnngh! I couldn't let that go. I should have – I could've come back to the party thing later – but I just couldn't stop myself.

"Actually, Matt got into trouble today."

"What for?"

"He was singing in our German lesson."

"Singing? Why was he singing?"

"Oh, because there's this German exchange thing that no one wants to go on, and he thought it was funny. Anyway. . ."

"There's a German exchange going on? When?"

"In a couple of months, I think. So. . ."

"That'd be really good practice for you."

"Hang on, I don't want to—"

"I think that's a really good idea. Isn't that a good idea?"

I took one look at my mum, and realized that she'd forgotten all about Matt, or parties. All she'd heard were the words German exchange – and if it was going to be Good For My Education, I was going. End of discussion. Even if it meant inviting a crazy German into her house. She was probably already mentally making sleeping arrangements. Her last comment was directed at my dad, who looked up from rearranging his CDs.

"Hmm? Yes. As long as he doesn't start annexing the neighbours."

Scheisse.

"When's the deadline?" My mum turned back to me.

"What?"

"Well, you've probably left it until the last minute to tell me about this, haven't you?"

"No." Well, no point making her panic.

"So I think you should probably tell Miss Spencer you're going the next time you've got a lesson with her. I just hope she's got a few places left."

"Yeah. OK." Maybe, if I was lucky, fifty people might volunteer first thing tomorrow. Still, I wouldn't be counting on it. My arm was bleeding,

I was supposed to be having a party with no guests and no cool stuff, and I'd just talked myself into getting shipped off to Germany. I plodded upstairs – but as I did, a plan started to form.

From: dylan25@hotmail.com
To: rudi@heidelbergschule.org.de

Hi Rudi!
I am writing to invite you to stay with us – I expect your teacher has told you about the exchange trip. It's in February, so remember to pack an umbrella if you're coming – it will probably rain all month. On the plus side, the traditional English football hooliganism is not so popular at that time of year, so you'll probably get away without any trouble. I hope you can come – it would be nice to have someone to practise my kickboxing with.
Tchuss
Dylan

If I couldn't avoid inviting the psycho to stay with us, I'd just have to make sure he wouldn't want to. With any luck he'd send me a reply declining my polite invitation and I'd be able to delete my original message before I showed it to Miss Spencer and my mum. I just hoped he didn't wonder why I hadn't mentioned my kickboxing before. I ran the message through freetranslation.com — it didn't seem to know the word for "hooliganism", but never mind — and clicked Send, and I was just mentally congratulating myself for being a genius when I noticed my Inbox flashing.

From: qui_gon_jinn6@hotmail.com
To: dylan25@hotmail.com

Dude!
You'll never guess what's happened! I've met a girl! I was going to tell you the other day, but I didn't want to do it at school in case someone overheard us ;) She's into all the same stuff as me – her tag's Mangagirl, and she knows all about Dragon Ball Z and Yu-Gi-Oh and stuff. I might even ask her to meet up with me next time I mail her. No idea who it is – didn't think any girls from our school were into that stuff. Maybe someone

from another year? Who sez I spend too much time on the net?
Laterz
Will

I stared at the screen for a long time – well, probably only about two minutes – until Becky shouted something about needing to use the phone. Then I just sat slumped over in my chair for a while.

For as long as I could remember, Will was sort of my insurance policy when it came to girls. He wasn't that bad-looking, or even that geeky, but he just didn't *try*. No, Will was safe. Whoever else was attached/snogging/getting married, I reckoned, at least I'd be ahead of Will. And now Will had a girlfriend. OK, so she was an online cyber-girlfriend that he'd never even seen – but still, the only person I had to e-mail was Rudi. Things were going from bad to wurst.

Single White E-mail

"Could've been Sarah," I suggested.

"Nah. She ran away during the whole mistletoe thing last year, and said she never wants to see the little creep again," Dec pointed out.

It was Thursday morning. It was breaktime. I'd managed to stay angry at Dec about the skatepark incident for, ooh, nearly a whole hour before I gave up and started talking to him again. I'd managed to convince myself that the disastrous "date" wasn't really Dec's fault — well, apart from the T-shirt thing, anyway. Of course, it might've been something to do with the fact that I had other things to worry about — like Will's virtual reality girlfriend.

"Rachel?"

"I don't think Rachel can even work a

computer," Dec snorted. "Besides, there's no way she'd be e-mailing Will. I mean, what about Matt, for a start. . . No. Hannah?"

"No," I said, thinking about the way Hannah refused to even come near us when Will was around.

"Charlotte?"

"Doubt it."

"That new girl?"

"No!" I said, a bit too loud. "I mean, Kate hasn't even spoken to Will yet."

"Oh, sorry – Kate, is it? You fancy her, do you?"

"Shut up."

"So that's a yes, then."

"No," I spluttered. "Well, maybe a bit."

"Well, think of her like your Man United. You're going to need at least a warm-up match."

"What?"

"Look, I don't care if you don't fancy Fiona," Dec said, generously. "As long as you're still up for being my wingman."

"What? No, shut up," I said. "I'm not going to. . . Look, can we *please* just get back to Will for a minute?"

The trouble was, even between the two of us

we weren't having much luck working out who Mangagirl was. It had to be someone from our school, because otherwise they wouldn't be able to get on to the message board – so at least we knew it wasn't a weirdo or a lonely old lady or something. The trouble was, girls just didn't *use* the school message board – it was for Will and his weird mates to talk about (in theory) homework and (more likely) computer games. It wasn't that the girls in my year *couldn't* use computers, it was just that . . . well, it was just that most people had better things to do with their time than flirt on them. Of course, most people didn't have Will's mum to deal with. Remember how I mentioned that she doesn't approve of Dec and me very much? Well, imagine how she feels about the rest of the world – girls included – and then think about how keen she is on letting her precious son go out in the big, bad world. At least in his bedroom, the worst thing that could happen to Will is the *Millennium Falcon* falling on his head.

Another thing we weren't having much luck with was the party. Somehow, the fact that I really fancied Kate actually kept making it harder to talk to her, as if something important was shutting down as soon as I got within three metres of her. That meant I wasn't risking inviting her to the party just yet, in case I just broke down and started drooling when I gave her the invitation. Apart from that, the rest of the week crawled by, but it was mostly taken up by being really bored (in lessons), trying to avoid looking anywhere in the general direction of Matt and Rachel (at breaktimes) and sitting in Admiral Ackbar's detentions (for Dec). By Saturday afternoon, I still hadn't got around to telling Miss Spencer about me going on the German exchange, managed to find out who Will's mystery girlfriend was, or had *any* ideas about "something special" to do. Dec, it turned out, hadn't done much better.

"I've been thinking," he said, blowing bubbles in a strawberry frappuccino. I squinted at the magazine he was waving in front of my face. He'd said he wanted a "planning meeting" in the coffee shop, but if this was his idea of a plan . . . well, I wasn't very impressed.

"What," I said. "The *hell*. Is *that*?"

"It's like one of those mechanical rodeo bulls." Dec explained, excitedly. "Except it's a sheep! Isn't it brilliant?"

I looked at the page again.

"I don't think they'd hire one of those out to a thirteen year old," I said. "And it's probably a bit expensive."

"OK. . ." Dec carried on. "Plan B. Remember *Charlie's Angels*? The bit where the bad guy and Bill Murray dress up as sumo wrestlers? I think you can *hire* them. The costumes, I mean. That'd be brilliant."

"But you'd look like a sumo wrestler," I pointed out.

"So?"

"Well, I'm not sure girls like sumo wrestlers. They wouldn't even be able to get their arms round you." I pictured my first kiss with Kate happening while I was dressed up with an enormous fake stomach. She wouldn't be able to get *near* me.

"You wouldn't be wearing them all the time. . ." said Dec.

"I think we need something a bit cheaper," I insisted.

"Like what?" Dec looked exasperated.

"Um. . . Twister?" I suggested.

"Twister's crap."

"Yeah."

"So we need –" Dec started ticking off his

fingers — "an idea that's a) cheap, b) easily accessible to teenagers, c) fun and d) not completely crap."

"Tricky," I said.

"Mmm," agreed Dec. "Also, I think we should invite Natalie and Fiona."

I nearly choked on my cappuccino.

"No. Nonono. No way."

"Come on," Dec said. "This was all part of the plan."

"Not my plan." I folded my arms. "I'm not asking them."

"Fiona really liked you," said Dec.

"Really? Because, you know, when she was completely ignoring me, I *thought* she was probably just playing hard to get."

"She told Natalie she liked you."

"That's such an obvious lie. Give me a bit of credit."

It looked as if one "date" hadn't been enough to separate Natalie from her limpet-like mate.

"Look, do me a favour."

I felt bad for him, I really did.

"No."

"Come on."

"No. Absolutely, definitely not."

I'd made my mind up. I was actually quite proud of how firm I was being. Unfortunately, that wasn't going to be enough.

"Hii-eeeee!"

Oh no.

"Over here!"

Dec. It could have been coincidence, of course, that Fiona and Natalie just *happened* to wander into the same coffee shop as us. Just like it *could* have been coincidence that Dec had happened to wear a T-shirt under his school gear on Wednesday. In other words, I'd been set up. Again.

"Dylan! How are *yooouu*? I haven't seen you for *aaages!*" Fiona shouted across the room. Maybe it was all the normal people around her, but this time she looked even madder than she did at the skatepark. I had a terrible feeling about this.

Something was different this time, though. For a start, Fiona slumped down at our table right next to me and grabbed my arm, as if she absolutely had to know how I was. The last time we'd met, she'd hardly spoken to me. And now? Well. . .

Sorry for changing the subject here, but before my sister started being a hippy – this was a couple of years ago – she used to read *Cosmopolitan*, the girliest of the grown-up girl mags. Seriously,

70

there was this huge teetering stack of them in her room, until she got all PC and recycled the whole lot because they were a "celebrity-obsessed waste of trees". Which was a bit of a problem for me, because they're pretty interesting reading if you're trying to work out how girls' brains work. And one thing that *Cosmo* does all the time is How to Flirt guides, which tend to be full of advice on how to work out whether someone's interested in you or not. Useful stuff, if you're trying to work out what the hell the skater girl opposite you's playing at:

1. Eye Contact. Loads. Fiona was staring at me like she was expecting me to sprout an extra head. She seemed to be having a bit of trouble focusing, but maybe she wore contact lenses, or something.
2. Touching. Again, loads. She kept patting, stroking or squeezing my arm, which, according to *Cosmo*, is a Sure Thing.
3. Smiling/Laughing. Absolutely tons. Her and Natalie actually started laughing when Dec went "How are you, ladies?" Bizarre.
4. Fidgeting with Hair. Well, none, actually. But I thought the other three were pretty conclusive.

What was going on? Had I suddenly become much more attractive without realizing it? True, I wasn't wearing my school uniform this time, but . . . hang on.

"God, I've had *such* a boring day," sighed Fiona. Why was she smelling of apples? "Have *you* had a good day?"

Don't tell me. . .

"Have you been drinking?" I said. Good grief, I sounded like my mum.

"A *little* bit," said Fiona, making the universally accepted symbol for "tiny thing" – a finger and thumb close together – and giggling as if I'd just said something hilariously cheeky. She put her head on my shoulder. "Where've you *been* all day?"

"Just hanging out," I said, playing it safe.

"That's cool," said Fiona, going all big-eyed and nodding. This was starting to drive me mad.

Suddenly, Natalie was tugging at Dec's arm. "Let's go to the skaaatepaaark," she said, in that whiny tone of voice you're only supposed to use when you're six years old and your mum's refusing to take you to Alton Towers. "Come ooooon."

Dec gave me a sort of pleading look. The

scowling waitress gave us another frown. "Well. . ."
I started.

After ten minutes of walking along with Fiona
clumping alongside me and hanging on to my
arm, she got bored of laughing insanely and
scooted up to talk to Natalie. Dec dropped back
to chat to me.

"I think they're hammered," he said.

"I know."

"Brilliant, eh?" He gave me a smirk.

"What? Why?"

"Oh, come on – did you even *see* the way
Fiona's looking at you? You're practically
guaranteed a snog."

"Oh, yeah. Brilliant. I'm 'practically guaranteed
a snog' with an obvious nutcase. You're phoning
the ambulance if she bites my tongue off."

"Don't be such a spoilsport. She seems lovely."

We tramped on in silence.

By the time we got to the skatepark, I wasn't
even sure why we were there. I mean, even if
they were impressed by Dec's two tricks, he
didn't actually have his board with him.

Then Fiona and Natalie started waving
frantically. But not at us.

"Hiii-eeee! Banksy! Hii-eee!"

And they were off, sprinting towards the grass verge.

"Banksy", it turned out, was a bloke. Well, practically a bloke. He looked about eighteen, but he had that world-weary, seen-it-all look that people who sit in parks all day seem to get. He was wearing a baseball cap and smoking – and to be honest, he looked a bit like a rat. In fact, he was exactly the sort of person you wouldn't go anywhere near if your best mate wasn't shoving you in the back.

"Banksy, Rob, Endo, this is Dylan and Declan."

Rob and Endo, it turned out, were nearer our age – but still about sixteen or seventeen – and wearing exactly the same sort of hoodies as Fiona and Natalie. It must be great when you're that rebellious.

"Hey," mumbled Rob.

"'Sup," growled Endo.

"All right, girls?" grinned Banksy. I sat down, trying not to make it too obvious that I was putting as much space between myself and him as humanly possible.

"Anyway, how're youuu?" said Fiona, sitting

herself right in the middle of the group. "I haven't seen you for aaaages!"

"Ahh, y'know, girls, just been chillin' and that," said Banksy. He even *sounded* a bit like a rat.

Before long, the girls were chatting happily away. Banksy didn't say much, and the most Rob and Endo ever managed was a "huh" or "yeah", but Natalie and Fiona didn't seem that bothered. Dec occasionally tried to join in the conversation with a laugh or a "yeah, right" but he obviously felt upset about not being the centre of attention any more. Finally, Banksy seemed to notice us.

"Either of you want a drink?" He waved a bottle of weird purplish stuff at us. It didn't look like any drink I'd ever seen — I mean, for a start, it seemed to be in an old milk carton. I'd seen everyone else taking the occasional glug out of it, but judging by the way they were all acting, I wasn't sure that meant it was a good idea.

"What is it?" said Dec.

"Ribena," said Endo. Rob and the girls laughed.

"Here you go, mate," said Banksy, screwing the lid back on and chucking the carton to Dec. Dec hesitated for a second, then took a sip so tiny it probably evaporated before it hit his throat, and made a face. Everyone laughed.

"Dylan?" He offered the bottle to me.

"No, thanks. I'm trying to cut down."

"Go on," said Fiona, grinning.

"No, really, I'm fine. Look, there's hardly any left. You have it, if you want." Even *I* knew how stupid that sounded – the carton was still more than half full.

"Go ooon."

Fiona was hugging my arm with what looked to me like an evil glint in her eye. It was cider, I decided. It *had* to be cider. Some weird, purple type of cider that they'd made out of grapes, or something, instead of apples.

"Go ooooon."

I decided to take one big swig and then refuse to do any more. My brother could drink *pints* of cider. How bad could it be? One, two three:

Swiiiiig. . .

"Bleuurchh!"

It wasn't cider.

Purple just isn't a colour that *works* for me. I don't own any purple T-shirts, and I certainly haven't got any purple trousers. If I ever went on a makeover TV show – not that I want to – I'd probably flat-out refuse to wear any purple.

Which is why it was a bit embarrassing when I half-spat, half-spilled about a litre of purple home brew down the front of my shirt after my over-enthusiastic attempt to chug back the mystery drink. It was mainly surprise, I think, because whatever it was in the carton tasted a lot more like battery acid than anything I could see Lennon drinking (not that I've ever tried battery acid, but . . . well, you know). Rob, Endo and Banksy were annoyed because I'd wasted most of their home-brewed madness juice, Fiona and Natalie thought it was hilarious and Dec just pretended not to notice when I suddenly remembered that I had to dash off home. And now, I was walking the long walk back to my house alone, wet, embarrassed and wearing a mostly-purple T-shirt. What a perfect time for Kate to turn up.

"Hey!"

She was across the road, waving at me. Even out of uniform, in combats and a jacket, I'd have recognized her anywhere – same nice hair, same brilliant smile. She looked gorgeous.

I'm only slightly ashamed to say that I

panicked a bit at this point. On the plus side, I was away from school, and therefore not at risk of ridicule, *friendus interruptus* or sudden attack by an Idiot. On the minus side, I looked like a big, berry-smeared baby. Then again, I couldn't exactly ignore her – she'd seen me, and it'd be really rude. On the other hand, I wasn't feeling really up to witty, intelligent conversation. What to do? What to do? Handily, my brain picked that moment, the point I needed it more than ever before, to go into absolute shutdown.

Not even thinking about it, I waved back. She crossed the road to talk to me.

"Hi!"

"Hi."

"You're in my German class, aren't you? You sit behind me."

"Yeah!" I said, trying to look as if this was a really interesting observation – cheers, the *Cosmo* Guide to Flirting. "My name's Dylan."

"Yeah, I know!" Kate smiled again. "Like the singer."

"Or the rabbit from *The Magic Roundabout*," I added, practically kicking myself as soon as I'd said it. Kate gave me a little puzzled frown.

"Right." There was a pause. Then it was time for the thing I was dreading. . . "I like your T-shirt."

I glanced down at myself as if I'd only just noticed that I was covered in purple gunk.

"Thanks. It's . . . Ribena. It's sort of a 'modern art' thing." That's right, be funny. Good one.

"Do you always do that when you're drinking Ribena?"

"Oh, no, no no. I wasn't actually *drinking* it. . ."

I wasn't sure whether "messy drinker" was worse than "teen alcoholic", but I definitely had to think of something else. Then: inspiration.

"You know how Ribena cartons can explode when you blow into them?" She didn't look convinced. "Well, erm, it did. The carton. Exploded."

Kate gave me a funny look.

"Why were you blowing into a Ribena carton?"

"I wasn't blowing into a Ribena carton." Whoops. "Dec was. And some of it got on me."

"Wow. All that got on you? He must be *soaked*."

"He is. Absolutely drenched."

Kate was smiling at me now. Did I mention what a fantastic smile she's got? Oh, that's right, I did.

"Well, be careful. I wouldn't want you getting pneumonia in the name of art."

"Hmm. I should probably go home and change, in fact." I said, like the thought had just occurred to me. "See you."

"Bye." She smiled again. Did I mention. . .? Oh, right. She was already off, strolling along the street.

"Bye," I said to myself. *Nice one*, went my brain. *She can't resist you.*

Fortunately, by the time I got home, I'd had time to come up with a better story than the one I told Kate. The plan was: I was on the bus . . . I was drinking my Ribena, when *wham!* the driver screeched to a stop and I had to stop a pregnant woman, or maybe an old man – possibly more believable – from falling over. In the process of heroically leaping to the rescue, I splashed myself with good old friendly Vitamin C – certainly not half a bottle of home-made booze. Ta-daaa! That had everything. I was so pleased with that, in fact, that I was almost disappointed when I found out that I needn't have bothered.

When I got in, my mum and dad were having a "discussion" about the present list for Marie's wedding. "Discussions" are one step away from a proper argument, in that nobody actually shouts and everybody's pretending to be reasonable, but everybody's really angry and nobody wants to back down. I managed to sneak upstairs and change into my least favourite T-shirt (a huge bright red and blue Superman one that my sister got me for my last birthday), without anyone noticing, then crept back downstairs again. It's never very wise to disturb my parents mid-"discussion", in case they both turn on you.

"They've invited us to their wedding," my mum was saying.

"And that's nice of them," said my dad. "But it doesn't mean we have to furnish their house."

"It's a lovely toaster," said my mum.

"They're nice cushions."

"Don't be such a cheapskate."

Basically, this was the deal – cousin Marie and her boyfriend Paul were giving us a bit of cake and making us listen to a vicar, and in return, they expected everyone to *furnish their house*. Nothing on the wedding list was less than twenty quid, and we'd left it until the last minute to buy anything. My dad kept pointing out that it's the thought that counts, and suggesting we get them some embroidered sofa cushions (£19.99). My mum was saying Marie might be her only niece to get married, and she'd decided to get a toaster (£59.99). To be fair, she just "happened" to leave the Argos catalogue propped open to the toasters page and it is a brilliant toaster – it's chrome-plated, and it's got a defrost function, as well as a rack for warming muffins, bagels and croissants. But still – sixty quid! That's a lot of toasting. After another twenty minutes of arguing, my dad gave in, but pointed out that if Marie gets divorced we'd better get it back. At that point, with his usual dreadful timing, Lennon rang. I grabbed the phone, since my parents were still grumpily sniping at each other.

"How's university?" I asked, not really caring much one way or the other.

"Oh, you know. . ." Lennon said, breezily. "Loads of essays and stuff to do."

Translation: I'm doing as little as possible. I thought about asking if he'd ever tried chugging a mysterious purple drink, and if it was likely to do me any permanent damage, but I decided not to bother.

"I'll get Mum – she'll want to talk to you about your suit for next Saturday."

"I'm not wearing a suit on Saturday."

"So what *are* you going to wear?" Suddenly, I had visions of Lennon dressed in a traditional Scottish wedding kilt. Or maybe a bridesmaid's outfit.

"Well, I've hired out this sort of purple-sequinned waistcoat and some silver trousers. It's a bit flashy, but it'll go with the lighting."

"What, in the church?" I tried to imagine how my aunt would react to Lennon turning up in silver trousers. To be honest, it was sort of a frightening thought.

"Which church?"

"The one where the wedding is."

Click. Honestly, he lives in his own world.

"I can't go to a wedding on Saturday! I've got a performance!"

"A performance? Of what?"

There was a pause. I could almost *hear* my brother thinking. Finally, he came up with:

"A lecture."

"A performance of a lecture? Who has lectures on Saturdays?"

"It's a special one. Look, do you think there's any chance of me getting out of this thing?"

"You're on your own. I'll get Mum."

Mum was still fuming, even though she'd got her own way about the toaster. From the tone of her voice, I suspected that Lennon was going to be at the church on Saturday. Weird, though – I've never heard him so worried about missing a lesson before. Even one involving a purple waistcoat.

By Tuesday morning, I'd pretty much forgotten about the mystery of Lennon and the silver trousers. Obviously, it helped that I had two hours of pop videos full of skimpily dressed girls to watch on Sunday morning. And on Monday, obviously, I'd had worse things – like school – to worry about. But the day after that, it was looking increasingly unlikely that I'd get struck down by a contagious (and not-too-harmful) virus, before Saturday – and I'd started to think about the wedding again.

"What're you going to do when *you* get married?" Will asked. It was breaktime, and I'd mentioned getting dragged to the wedding in a sort of *oh-poor-me* way. Of course, I'd forgotten that Will was actually *interested* in what you might call "romance" now.

"Dunno." Dec thought about it for a second,

then looked as if he'd been struck by inspiration. "Actually, I think you can get married underwater now."

"But then you have to marry someone who can swim." I pointed out. "Or a fish."

"Or a mermaid," added Will.

"Shut up, Will. Seriously, though, I don't think I'll ever get married," said Dec. "It sounds like too much hassle."

"Elvis," Will said, suddenly. "I'm going to get married by an Elvis impersonator. In Vegas."

"Really?" Dec turned to grin at him. "To who?"

"Dunno. . ."

Maybe it's because they don't always agree on everything, but Will doesn't always trust Dec very much. Dec already knew about Mangagirl – mainly because I'd told him – but as far as Will knew, it was still our little secret.

"I'm going to get married during a bungee jump," I said, changing the subject as quickly as possible. "I saw it on TV – you just leave the vicar on the ground and sort of say your vows while you're bouncing."

"I'm not sure many girls'd go for that." Will frowned.

"Yeah, but I'm going to marry Kirsten Dunst,"

I explained. "She's used to it. From *Spider-Man*."

"Hmm. . ." Dec started. "I think maybe that was a stuntwoman."

The plus side of having stupid conversations like this, of course, was that we didn't have to think about organizing the party. The downside, unfortunately, was that . . . well, that no one was organizing the party. I was starting to wonder if it was a good idea at all – after all, since all the It girls seemed to like the Idiots so much, maybe they'd just refuse to come. My brain was still being too unreliable for me to even *think* about asking Kate face to face, and after embarrassing myself in front of Fiona for the second time in a fortnight, I didn't even have a second-division friendly (Dec's words) to fall back on. And even though Will's "girlfriend" was just a collection of smileys on a screen, at least he *had* one – which was why I couldn't exactly bring myself to talk to him about the disaster with Fiona. Dec was obviously thinking about the same thing, because the next thing he said was:

"So what about those internet marriages?"

"What?" said Will, suddenly caught off guard.

"You know, those people who meet each other on the net, then dash off to Russia or whatever to get married, except they've never seen each other. What happens if you end up with an absolute stinker? Or maybe she's sent you a photo of herself, but it's from when she was ten years younger, or something? I mean, do you still go through with it? Or—"

"I *HATE* YOU!"

Everyone spun around – not that there was much point. After all, there's only one person who's that loud, let alone prepared to shout in a classroom. *Rachel.* She was standing in front of the Idiots, who'd briefly stopped their game of smack-each-other-on-the-knuckles-with-a-pack-of-cards to smirk at her amateur dramatics.

"You're *such* a child." Rachel was practically turning red. "I don't know why I ever . . . ooh!"

She stormed out, risking the anger of any nearby teachers by slamming the door so hard that the glass juddered. Karen and Hannah glared at Matt, then followed her – although they were a bit gentler with the door. The Idiots started giggling before it even closed.

"Muppets," muttered Dec.

"Hmm." I nodded.

It looked like Rachel and Matt's On/Off relationship was Off again, but I wasn't as pleased about it as I'd normally have been. After all, it might put the rest of the It girls off Matt for a while, but he was back in the game — and maybe he wanted his next fixture to be with Kate. . .

Dressing to Impress

I'm not in, mouthed my mum.

"She's not in," I said down the phone.

"Oh, that's a shame," said Aunt Jess. "I'll have to. . . Actually, you can tell her, can't you? Just tell your mum that the plates are going to be blue, will you, Dylan? Think you can manage that?"

"I. . . No problem." It's never a good idea to question my aunt. Even if it sounds like she's talking in code.

"Thanks, sweetheart. Bye!"

"She says," I said, hanging up the phone, "that the plates are going to be blue. It sounded very important."

"What?" said my dad and my sister together.

"I think," said my mum, "she's worried that our dresses aren't going to match the dishware."

"Aren't they?" said my dad, trying to look as if he even vaguely cared.

"*Dresses?*" said my sister.

"To be honest, I'm not too worried whether they do or not," my mum said to my dad. She turned to Becky, looking harassed. "Yes, you're wearing a dress."

"No, I'm not." Becky looked outraged. "Spider says he isn't going to wear a suit."

"*Spider*," said my mum, with a long-suffering look, "isn't going. He hasn't been invited."

"They're probably worried about his piercings not matching the cutlery," I pointed out. My dad did a little snort. Becky gave me one of her non-Buddhist looks and stormed out. And, of course, my mum said:

"*Dylan!*"

"Sorry."

Honestly, I don't know when to shut up. I just don't.

It had been like this all week. Every day, we were getting a call reminding us what time the ceremony kicked off (as if we'd forget), asking us if Becky couldn't just eat the fish to make things easier for everyone (no, she couldn't), or if Lennon was coming (yes, said my mum, in a tone that made it sound like he'd live to regret it if he didn't).

You had to give Aunt Jess one thing – she was organized. In fact, if she'd been less bothered about things like plates and dresses, I'd have thought about asking her to help out with our party. Apart from a couple of "meetings" where we hadn't come up with any good ideas (Dec wanted to make piñatas until he realized that it'd take about a day to stick together one papier-mâché pig), we hadn't done anything. It didn't help that Will seemed to be spending more and more time on his computer – either "talking" to Mangagirl or waiting for her to turn up. In fact, I tried ringing him late on Thursday night, and his phone was engaged, so I tried his mobile. He picked it up after two rings.

"Hello, mate. Er, can I ring you back?"

"Yeah, if you're . . . hang on, what are you doing?"

"I'm working."

"On a computer?"

"Yeah."

"Is that why your phone's engaged?"

"Um . . . yeah."

"So when you say 'working', you actually mean 'posting messages to a girl you've never met'."

"Maybe."

"Are you going to ask her to the party?"

"Maybe."

I hung up, natch. Two days to go until the wedding, and I *still* hadn't even managed to get a sudden outbreak of flu. . .

Going to the Chapel

"Ladies and gentlemen," said some bloke in a suit I'd never met before. "I think you'll find that there is no mud on my friend's trousers, he couldn't possibly have climbed that fence, and I can personally testify that he's afraid of sheep."

"*What?*" said my mum and sister together. My dad just raised an eyebrow. My aunt, up at the top table, looked like she was about to choke on a lump of salmon.

"Sorry, folks," grinned Suit Bloke, with what he seemed to be hoping would look like a cheeky wink. "Seeing Paul in a suit made me think we were in court again."

Groan.

Who doesn't love a wedding, eh? Catching bouquets, wearing a big hat, posing for six million photos, telling the vicar it was a lovely service — brilliant. Well, brilliant if you're my aunt, but actually pretty boring if you're me. *Nothing interesting at all* happened during the actual church bit. There was no getting-to-the-church-on-time drama, because everyone set off early on purpose. Nobody sprinted in during the "does anyone here know of any just impediment. . ." bit, because my cousin doesn't have any madly passionate ex-boyfriends. And now, just to top things off, the best man had decided to use the reception to work on his stand-up comedy routine.

"I'd like to take this opportunity to tell some stories about what Paul was like when I first met him," he carried on, vaguely waving at my cousin's new husband, "but I can't, on the advice of my legal team."

Groan.

I glanced around the room. The reception was taking up most of what was actually a pretty nice hotel restaurant, with proper doilies on the tables and an *enormous* cake. Up at the bride and groom's table with my aunt were some equally horrified-looking strangers — probably the groom's parents — and my uncle Frank, who actually seemed to be enjoying himself. Then again, since I wasn't allowed to get drunk and shout at people, I couldn't exactly copy *him*. I was sitting at one of the lower-down tables with my mum, dad, Lennon, and a very moody-looking Becky. Lennon, who'd turned up at home at eight o'clock on Friday night and immediately gone out with his mates until two-ish, was yawning.

"But seriously, Paul." The best man looked oblivious to the glares he was getting from everyone else at his table — Paul included. "It was a great stag night . . . and don't forget that twenty quid you owe me for those dances."

Groan.

The only person who seemed to be actually laughing was a frizzy-haired forty-something woman sitting at one of the tables opposite. She was swigging something that didn't look like water, and occasionally giggling like mad and nudging the very grumpy-looking girl next to her. I had no idea who the frizzy-haired woman was, but I couldn't help getting the feeling that I'd seen the grumpy girl before. . .

"So judging by the amount of pillows the staff are bringing in, that's enough from me," said the best man. Lennon did a little sarcastic cheer. "So I hope you'll all join me in a toast to the bride and groom."

"Bride and groom!" repeated Uncle Frank, a bit too enthusiastically.

There was a sort of collective sigh of relief, and everyone clinked glasses.

"Wasn't it a lovely service?" trilled my auntie Jess, whoomphing down into a spare chair near our table. Uncle Frank sagged into the chair next to her, and immediately commandeered the nearest bottle of wine.

"Yes," said my mum, not very enthusiastically.

"Mmm," agreed my dad.

"Yeah," said Becky, Lennon and me.

"Have you seen the cake properly yet?" Aunt Jess was really kicking things into high gear.

"Mm – isn't it lovely?" My mum was obviously starting to get bored now – my dad didn't even bother answering. Aunt Jess still had one last line to try, though.

"Didn't Marie look beautiful?"

Lennon covered his mouth with his hand and made a noise that sounded like "Pffft." It was true that Marie looked a bit, um, meringue-ish, but I couldn't help thinking that he was just jealous. After all, he'd obviously been bullied into turning up in a suit instead of his purple trousers. My mum gave him a "watch it" look and turned back to Aunt Jess.

"Yes, I was saying how lovely she looked."

It was about this time my dad decided to open the second bottle of wine. It looked like he was planning to give Uncle Frank a run for his money. My aunt decided to change tack.

"So . . . how's Dylan doing at school? How're you doing at school, Dylan?"

"All right." I mumbled, thinking about German exchanges, Idiots, Miss Spencer and Kate.

"Are you still on the rugby team?" tried Uncle Frank. At least he was making the effort, even if he seemed to be on a different planet.

"No. I, um, still hate rugby."

Honestly, when it comes to polite after-dinner conversation, I should just shut up and stuff my face with chocolate mints.

"Dylan's going on a German exchange soon. Aren't you, Dylan?" said my mum, giving me a little frown.

"Well, yeah, I mean, it's not definite yet. . ." I started.

"Why, what did your teacher say?" My mum turned around to give me one of her warning glances.

"Well. . ." I started, but Uncle Frank came to my rescue.

"What d'you want to go to Germany for? It's all lederhosen and sausages. Mind you. . ." he added, having another swig of wine, "I wouldn't mind going to that beer-tasting festival, you know, the what's-its-name. . ."

"Oktoberfest," mumbled Lennon.

"Oktoberfest!" carried on Uncle Frank, looking pleased with himself. "But I suppose you're a bit young for that, Dylan, hohoho."

"Yeah. . ." I mumbled, thinking that I probably ought to introduce Uncle Frank to Matt. Aunt Jess decided that everyone had wasted enough time on me.

"So how are *you*, Becky? Been to any riots recently? Ah-hahaha."

My sister was still upset that Spider hadn't been invited. I wasn't convinced that making fun of her political convictions was the best way to go.

"I think you mean protest marches," she said, coldly. "And no, I haven't, because *some people –*" (pointed stare at my dad) – "think I should be more worried about my French homework than who's running the country."

"I just think—" started my dad — but Uncle Frank, cheerfully joining the argument, wasn't going to give him a chance.

"I don't know why you bother. Politicians are all the bloody same anyway, aren't they?"

"I . . . it . . . but . . . you can't just. . ." You know how sometimes somebody says something so stupidly illogical that there's no way to argue with it? My sister gets that *all the time*. It must get pretty depressing.

"I mean," Uncle Frank was obviously starting to enjoy this heavyweight political debate, "look at the mess this lot're making of the universities. You can't honestly tell me that what's-his-face in the opposition'd be doing it any different."

"But he's a Tory!" exploded Becky. "Of *course* it'd be worse! We can't let, erm, you know, the Tories run our education system."

"Why not? Come to think of it, who's the shadow education secretary?" said Aunt Jess.

"Good question," said my mum.

There was a pause. Eventually, Lennon realized everyone was looking at him.

"I don't know," he said. "I do political *philosophy*."

"What's the difference, exactly?" asked Becky. I think she was relieved to have found someone she could actually have a proper argument with. Still, Lennon breezed that one.

He stared at her, totally unfazed, and explained:

"Political *science* is about the practise of government. Political *philosophy*'s about the theory of government. Like, you know, famous political thinkers through the ages, and stuff."

Becky wasn't letting that go.

"Right. So what d'you think of Plato's contention that we're basically all sitting in a cave and our experiences are just shadows on a wall?"

"I think he's right," said Lennon, not even blinking.

"Really?"

"Yes."

Things sort of got worse from that point on.

Lennon left the table as soon as he could, and dashed over to the nearest group of bridesmaids. Becky carried on her political debate with Aunt Jess and Uncle Frank, but she seemed to be getting more and more frustrated about them treating her like a six year old. My mum and dad joined in occasionally, but mostly just chatted amongst themselves. Sometime around the point my sister called Uncle Frank a fascist, I mumbled something about needing to go to the toilet and decided to make a run for it.

The trouble was, there wasn't anywhere to go – just other tables full of relatives I didn't want to talk to. There were only four people on the dancefloor – three doing that embarrassed shuffle-a-bit-and-don't-look-at-anyone dance, and the speech-loving woman from earlier shaking her frizzy hair about and waving her arms. I was just thinking about my chances of hiding in the toilets for the rest of the evening, when I noticed the grumpy girl again.

Who *was* she? From her clothes, she probably couldn't have been anyone from my school – even on non-uniform days, not many people wear black cocktail dresses and trainers. She looked a bit too old for school, of course, but that could've been the dress as well – or the glass of something that looked like lemonade, or the fact that she hadn't smiled all evening. Unfortunately, I must have spent too long staring at her while I was trying to work out the mystery, because before I knew it she was marching towards me. And up close, with the gallons of mascara scrubbed off and the pink hair extensions gone, it was obvious where I *really* knew her from. Except that the last time she'd seen me, I'd been covered in purple gunk and dashing in the opposite direction. Perfect.

"Hi, Fiona," I said, trying to look cheerful. Or at least, trying to look as if the worst night of my life wasn't just getting worse and worse.

"Stop staring at me." Somehow, Fiona seemed even grumpier up close.

"Um, OK."

"I've had enough of wearing this stupid outfit. I can do without people leching over me all night as well."

"But I wasn't, erm – you know. . . I like your trainers."

"Yeah, right." Fiona snorted.

"Enjoying the wedding?" I tried, realizing too late how stupid that sounded.

"No."

"Oh."

"I hate weddings. My mum reckons these two'll probably be divorced in five years anyway."

"Which one's your mum?"

"The one dancing."

The way she said *dancing*, I decided that her mum was probably the one waving her arms about as if she was signalling for help.

"Oh."

"She's friends with Jess."

"Oh."

"Between you and me. . ." she beckoned me towards her so she could whisper into my ear, ". . .I think she might be a little bit drunk." She said it with a little sneer in her voice, and I could sort of understand why — looking at the frizzy-haired woman, I thought "a little bit" was a bit of an understatement.

"Erm . . . right."

"What're *you* doing here, anyway?" Fiona suddenly looked suspicious, as if I'd deliberately sneaked in just to stalk her.

"Aunt Jess. . . I mean, Jess is my aunt."

"Hmm. What about that idiot?" She jerked her head at Lennon, who'd moved on to juggling fruit in the middle of his crowd of bridesmaids.

"He's my brother," I said, shaking my head.

"I know how you feel." Fiona nibbled at one of the little quiche things from the buffet, then made a face and threw it in the bin. "I'm bored. Fancy a dance?"

"No, thanks," I said, imagining how my mum and dad and – well, my entire family – might react to seeing me dancing with an obviously mad girl.

"Tough. Come on – I want to dance, and I don't want any of those other weirdos coming near me."

Fiona grabbed my hand so that I practically had no choice except to follow her towards the DJ's little booth – occupied by a bored-looking thirtyish bloke with greasy-looking hair that he had to keep sweeping out of his eyes. She stood on tiptoe to whisper something in his ear, and pretty soon he was grinning and rummaging around in his record bag. Fiona was already dragging me on to the dancefloor when, suddenly, a thrashy-rock number blasted out of the speakers.

"Brilliant!" I heard Lennon say, pulling the nearest bridesmaid on to the dancefloor. "It's The Darkness!"

Yeah, brilliant. Except for one thing:

I Can't Dance.

No, seriously. That sort of glued-together

shuffle you do at the end of an evening? I had a go at that once, and I didn't tread on the girl's feet, so that's all right. Standing on the edge of a dancefloor with my arms folded, bobbing my head? I'm a *genius* at that. But once I start actually moving my arms and legs in time with the music, I start thinking about how I must look, and once I do that I slow down, and that only makes it worse and then I just sprint off the dancefloor. I just can't dance. And Fiona could. And she was miles better than her mum.

The thing was, like her mum, she obviously didn't care about the people staring at her, but unlike her mum, she was actually pretty coordinated – although the trainers probably helped. Besides, there weren't very many people in her way for very long, because the grungy-pop number she'd chosen was driving everyone off the dancefloor. The DJ rocked on for as long as he could, but when the best man started to march over to his box, he scratched out Fiona's rock track halfway through and put on some cheesy 70s number that I about half-recognized. People started creeping back on to the dancefloor, but Fiona wasn't giving up that easily.

"Come on!" she shouted, grabbing my arms — so I didn't really have a choice in the matter. With someone pulling on your arms, you actually look stupider trying to stand still than moving the rest of your body, so I pretty much had to sway at least vaguely in time until Fiona let go. The next song was an Elvis tune I recognized as one of my dad's favourites, so it was easier to dance to that. During the third song I remembered that my entire family was probably laughing at me, so I tried to sit down, but Fiona just grabbed my arms again.

The fourth song was a slow one.

I can't remember what it was, exactly — something by Frank Sinatra, I think — but before long, everyone who stayed on the dancefloor was doing the glued-together shuffle. Eep.

"I'm probably going to have a sit down, actually," I said to Fiona, in what seemed like a higher-pitched voice than normal. "I'm not feeling too great."

"Don't be daft," said Fiona. "It's just hot in here. Let's go and get some fresh air."

And before I knew it, she was dragging me off the dancefloor again. Lennon, pirouetting in the middle of a circle of bridesmaids, grinned, gave

me a thumbs-up and dropped into the splits – I didn't even know he could *do* that. Then Fiona was pulling me out of the room, down the hotel corridor and . . . into the girls' toilets.

"Feeling better?" She grinned at me, pulling me into the only unlocked cubicle and shutting the door.

"Um," I said, actually feeling even worse.

"You're actually quite cute when you're embarrassed." Fiona smirked, brushing a bit of hair out of my face and leaning towards me.

"Um," I said again, trying not to flinch.

My brain was going: *This is it. It's about to happen.* And another voice went: *Yeah, but is this seriously what you want? Look at her. What about Kate?* And then the first voice, much louder, went: *Shut up. Imagine how surprised Dec's going to be. Go for it. . .*

But then, another voice, which definitely wasn't coming from inside my head, went:

"Get out of the *way*, Fiona!"

And someone with a napkin over their mouth and a mass of frizzy hair tried to push past us into the cubicle.

But by then it was too late.

Blaaaaargh.

Party's Over

OK, so what happened in the girls' toilet wasn't exactly my fault. But the thing was, by the time I'd finished cleaning the worst of Fiona's mum's puke off my shoes, then explaining to my family how what was left of it wasn't mine, *then* explaining to them what I'd been doing in the girls' toilet, I sort of felt like I *was* partly to blame. It didn't help when, on her way out, Fiona stopped by our table and said:

"I've got to go. I think it'd probably be a good idea if we didn't speak to each other again."

And it *really* didn't help that Lennon spent most of the journey home complaining that we'd had to leave too fast for him to get the oldest bridesmaid's phone number. So, yeah, I spent most of Sunday sulking about that,

obviously. I'd have carried on through Monday, too – but by breaktime Dec had decided to cheer me up, and he wasn't taking "go away" for an answer.

"Girls, eh? She'll change her mind."

"Yeah, but I'm not sure I want her to," I said. "I mean, let's face it – every time I get near her, I end up ruining my clothes. I might just leave her alone from now on."

"Whatever. Just as long as you find someone to invite to the party."

"Yeah, well, I dunno about that."

"What's that supposed to mean?"

"I'm not sure this party thing's such a good. . ."

"Oh no. No, no no. Wait a minute." Dec frowned. "You're not just ditching it."

"I'm not saying I'm *ditching* it, I'm just. . ."

"You're not copping out on inviting a girl," Dec said, firmly.

"Why, who've you invited? That mad girl?"

"I've. . . I'm. . ." Dec looked slightly flustered. "I'm keeping my options open, all right? Anyway, we're talking about you."

"Well, I'm sort of running out of options, aren't I?"

"*And* you're supposed to be coming up with

something cool to do, remember?" Dec carried on.

"Hang on a minute, *I'm* supposed to be thinking of something?"

"Yeah." Dec looked disgruntled. "I've been organizing everything else."

"Oh, right, you've bought some Pringles," I muttered.

"Oh, yeah, sorry, that's right, I'm supposed to organize your *entire life* for you," Dec growled. "I've already tried setting you up twice, and you've managed to mess it up both times, I'm sorting a party so you and your *hopeless* mate have got a chance of getting near a real live girl. . ."

"Hang on. . ." I said, but Dec wasn't stopping.

"And you're sitting there feeling sorry for yourself because someone puked on your shoes!"

"Oh, as *if*," I shouted back. "You're not having this party for Will and me, you're having it because you're so desperate for a snog. I don't know why you're even bothering – you could just hang out at the skatepark and lech off people while you're pretending to be Tony Hawk!"

"Calm down, ladies," grinned Matt, strolling past.

"Get stuffed," muttered Dec, just too quietly for him to hear. "I can't *believe* you, Dylan. You're such a baby."

"Well, I suppose the party's off, then."

"Whatever."

"Fine."

Dec grabbed his bag and stormed off – and that was it. It looked like the party was over before it had even started. I mean, I was sure we'd sort it out eventually, but in time for Saturday? After he'd called me a *baby*? I'd only just managed to resist the urge to twang an elastic band at the back of his head.

To make things worse, my "hopeless" mate was having problems of his own.

"You want to get *rid* of all this stuff?" I said, staring around in disbelief.

With the skatepark off-limits in case I ran into Fiona, Dec or (aargh) Banksy, I'd decided to go round to Will's house to see how he was getting on with his mystery "girlfriend" and talk to him about the German exchange. It turned out that he'd been emotionally blackmailed into volunteering as well, although at least he hadn't volunteered first – Superboy Scott Forrester signed up ages ago. But anyway, Will didn't care very much that I wasn't speaking to Dec, or about getting landed with a crazy German penfriend – he had other things to worry about.

"Well, I've been meaning to for a while, really. I mean, it's not very grown up, is it?"

I was staring at Jango. And Count Dooku. And Daredevil, and Spider-Man, and Goku and all the other plastic men fighting their way across Will's room. It had taken him *years* to get them all together. And now, just like that, he was planning to chuck them away.

"So? Who cares?" I said. I wasn't feeling very grown up myself. Not if it meant getting shouted at and puked on.

"My mum's always going on at me about it."

Somehow, I couldn't see Will's mum suddenly telling him to grow up. She's the only mum I know who still brings glasses of orange squash up on a tray when her son's got friends round. Then, something occurred to me.

"This isn't because of that girl, is it?"

"Well. . ."

"*Is* it?"

"A bit," Will admitted. "She was saying she thinks toys are a bit . . . babyish. I mean, what happens if she comes round here and sees them?"

"She's coming round here?" I asked, slightly shocked.

"Well, not yet. . ."

"Have you even asked her to the party yet?"

"Well no. . ."

"Because I'd have to say, I'm not sure throwing all your stuff away for someone you haven't even met is a good idea."

"You don't think?"

"Don't be daft. I thought she was into this stuff, anyway."

"I suppose." Will looked sheepish.

"Maybe you should just ask her to the party, then, I don't know, decide once you've met her."

"Maybe."

Then, suddenly, a plan just popped into my head.

"Thinking about it, though – have you got any toys you don't *particularly* want?"

"Yeah, probably." Will shrugged. "Why?"

I explained, with plenty of arm-waving. Will started off looking a bit dubious. Then he started grinning. Then, half an hour later, I dashed out of

Will's house with my rucksack bulging. Another half-hour later – because I don't have a mobile phone (thanks, Mum) and I had to wait until I got home – I finally rang Dec to apologize.

"Mate, listen, sorry about earlier," I said. "No, that's cool . . . no, it was my fault, but listen . . . no, wait, just *shut up* for a second. I've got a brilliant idea. . ."

OK – I'll explain about my brilliant idea later, I promise. But in the meantime, all you need to know is: Dec loved it – and with The Plan sorted, all we had to do was organize the rest of the party. To be honest, that was fairly easy – Will was in charge of making the invitations, Dec was in charge of actually inviting people, I was in charge of making sure no Idiots turned up and we were all in charge of bringing crisps to stuff ourselves with. In fact, there was just one more thing I had to do. . .

Come on, went one bit of my brain. *What's the matter with you? It's easy – just go over there and ask her.*

No chance, went another bit. *What if she says no? You'll never live it down.*

"Are you going to ask her, or what?" Dec interrupted.

"In a minute," I stalled. "I'm just working out what to say."

Since I'd explained The Plan, Dec had totally forgiven me for calling him a lech, and I'd just about forgiven him for calling me a baby. He'd already invited about half of our year to the party, promising most of them that "something brilliant" was going to happen.

"Just *ask* her," he said. "You don't have to *say* anything."

"OK. Just give me a second."

I looked at the invitation in my hand. It was a bit crumpled, mainly because I was clenching it so tightly, but you could still make out Dec's address in the middle of a huge explosion. It looked pretty cool, but I couldn't help wondering if the little cartoon characters with huge eyes flying out of the cloud of smoke and debris were a deliberate attempt to impress *someone*. After all, Will designed them. . .

All right, I thought. *It's not as if you're asking her out. It's just a party. If she says no, you can just. . .*

"Oh, *I'll* ask her," said Dec, trying to snatch the mangled invitation off me.

"No!" I said. "Hang on. One second."

Right, my brain went. *Here we go. . .*

"Settle down, everyone!" called Miss Spencer, marching into the room. "Dylan, Chris, Keith — back in your seats."

Dang.

"Now," said Miss Spencer, once everyone was sitting reasonably quietly. Somehow, she seemed a bit less enthusiastic than usual. "Does *anyone* want to go on the German exchange? I need a final list soon, and if I don't get any names from this class, we might have to call the whole thing. . . Yes, Dylan?"

"Um. . ." I almost wanted to back out, but I couldn't. Ever since the wedding, my mum had made it pretty clear that if I didn't do *this* trip, I wouldn't be getting to do *any* other trips, ever. Even if my penfriend was crazy. ". . .I'd like to volunteer. I mean, I'd like to go on the German exchange."

A sort of murmur went through the classroom. Even from two desks back, I recognized Dec's groan.

"Woo!" Matt slapped me on the back just hard enough to be annoying. "*Schnell!*"

"Be *quiet*, Matt," said Miss Spencer. And then something weird happened. She actually *smiled* at me. "Well, that's excellent, Dylan. I can't tell you what a great opportunity this is for you, even if no one else. . ."

"Actually. . ." said Kate, sticking her hand up. "I'd like to go as well."

The murmur was louder this time – but Matt didn't say anything. In fact, he looked as if he'd been temporarily struck dumb.

"That's wonderful, Kate!" Miss Spencer actually looked *relieved*. "I'll give out the forms in a minute . . . unless there are any other takers? . . .No? Well. . ."

"Oh, I might as well," said Chris, shoving his hand in the air. "My mum'll be pleased, anyway."

"I'll go!" squeaked Hannah, glancing across at Chris. "It'll be fun!"

I'd never seen Miss Spencer so happy. By the time a couple more people had volunteered, she looked like she was practically crying with relief. After getting us to write down our names on her form – I was sort of surprised she didn't make us do it in our own blood – she finally started the lesson with a chirpy, "Right, books open at chapter twelve. . ."

Matt let out a massive groan right in my ear. It didn't bother me too much, though – in a weird way, he'd done us a favour by dumping Rachel and getting all the It girls angry at him for a week or so. They'd all agreed not to mention the party to any Idiots, and Dec was being extra careful not to invite anyone who'd spill the beans. As an added precaution, we hadn't actually put any details about The Plan on the invitations, just in case they fell into the wrong hands (teachers, parents, sensible people). Everything was going brilliantly. And it was about to get even better.

"Dylan!" Kate dashed up to me after the lesson. "You didn't tell me you were going on the German exchange."

"Yeah, well, it was sort of my mum's idea. . ."

"It's going to be great!" said Kate. "I thought I'd be the only one of our class to sign up."

Aargh.

"Yeah, definitely," I said. "Erm, I'm really looking forward to it. Um."

We both looked at the floor for a second.

"We should meet up sometime," said Kate, suddenly. My brain practically flipped over. "You know, to practise our German."

"Well. . ." I said, not exactly sure how to put it. "We're having a sort of . . . thing at Dec's on Saturday." I fished a very crumpled, slightly ripped invitation out of my pocket. "It's not ideal for, um, practising German, but you know, if you want to meet up. . ."

"A thing?" said Kate.

"Well, a party."

"Great!" Kate took the invitation. "I might see you there!"

Ye-es! Dylan: one – Idiots: nil!

"I asked her!" I told Will. "She's coming!"

Obviously, I'd played it fairly cool when I told Dec. After all, he wasn't that likely to be impressed – he'd already asked about a dozen girls to the party, and I had no idea which one was going to be his "date". But with Will – who is, remember, *much* worse at dealing with girls than me, well, I'd expected him to be at least a bit, erm, amazed. Which was why I was surprised when he just said:

"Oh, right. Well done."

"I mean, Kate's coming," I said, trying to get the point across.

"Good. So's Mangagirl." Will smiled.

"What?"

Will was grinning now. "I asked her. You sort of convinced me last night. And she said yes! I'm going to meet her at the party! I'm going to be carrying a lightsaber so she recognizes me."

I just looked at him, half-impressed (at Will's bravery) and half-horrified (at the thought of him carrying a plastic sword around).

"A lightsaber?" I said, thinking about the fact that this girl had just been telling him how childish she thought toys were.

"Right," Will carried on, unfazed. "I'm called Qui Gon Jinn, remember, so it makes perfect sense."

"Right. Yeah, of course. Perfect sense." I decided not to point out that carrying a lightsaber was probably the best way to avoid talking to any other girls for the entire evening. I didn't dare ask Will what he'd do if Mangagirl didn't turn up – I thought it might scar him for life. But I had to ask. . .

"What if she's really weird?" That seemed like a cheap shot, but I was actually a bit worried. What if Will got his hopes up and then some complete freak turned up? He'd be crushed.

"How can she be weird? She's into all the same stuff as me," Will said, as if I'd just asked the stupidest question in the world.

"Good point."

Now I was *really* worried.

Of course, just asking Kate to the party wasn't going to do me any good. I was probably going to have to talk to her while she was there as well, or something. Will obviously wasn't going to be any help unless I brought a keyboard and convinced her to chat via e-mail, and Dec . . . well, I didn't entirely trust Dec. So, with two nights to go, I'd decided to take the plunge and ring Lennon. After all, he was so . . . well . . . OK, so to be honest, he was hopeless when I was trying to come up with party ideas, and he was avoiding speaking to my mum after he'd done a backspin on the dancefloor and wrecked his suit. But I'd decided to give him another chance. I couldn't help remembering weird Lucy, his yoga-obsessed girlfriend. Or Kim, the kickboxer. Or Robin, the one with the skinhead hairdo and Japanese writing tattooed down her arms. Or. . . Well, OK, so Lennon's girlfriends weren't always perfect. But I mean, what else was I going to do? Talk to my dad?

"Hey, Mithter Tambourine Man. How'th it

going?" Lennon answered the phone after about two rings, sounding cheerful . . . and weird.

"All right. How're you?"

"Oh, you know – loadth of ethayth to do."

"Yeah . . . y'know when you . . . hang on a minute."

"What?"

"Why are you talking like that?"

I'll give him credit, though – he managed a pretty decent attempt at sounding surprised.

"Like what?"

"Like that."

There was a pause, while Lennon either decided he'd better tell the truth, or came up with the stupidest lie I've ever heard.

"Um . . . burnt my mouth while I wath fire-eating."

"What? What were you doing that for?"

"Trying to impreth thome girlth. Don't tell Mum –thhe thinkth I've got a cold."

I don't know what I'd been expecting, but it definitely wasn't that. Remember what I said about showing off in front of girls by doing stupid things? I was starting to think that for some people, it never wore off. Suddenly, I decided that I didn't really want Lennon giving me advice about girls any more. The trouble was, that only left one person I could think of who might be able to help me out. And I wasn't sure she'd want to. . .

"What do you *want*?"

Becky glared at me from her bed. Becky's room's a sort of shrine to everything "hippy" – mobile things with feathers sticking out of them, beanbags, beardy revolutionary leaders – I'm usually afraid to go in there in case I choke on the scented-candle fumes. She was holding some book or other about Buddhism, but I didn't feel like pointing out the contradiction between reading about being a pacifist and shouting at your relatives.

"I need some advice," I said.

"Right," Becky snorted, not even putting her book down.

"What's the appeal of stupid lads?"

"I don't like stupid lads." Great. She looked even angrier. "And I've told you not to talk about Spider like that."

Whoops.

"No, I mean, girls," I tried. "Why do you, girls, as a group, like stupid lads so much?"

"We don't."

"But you do, obviously," I pointed out. "Remember Matt? Half the girls in my class fancy him, and he's an absolute loser."

Becky thought about that for a second.

"Is he the one who goes around thumping people?"

I nodded.

"It's a rebellion thing. They only fancy him because he's a Bad Lad. They'll grow out of it." She went back to reading her book, with a triumphant "case closed" look on her face. I thought about Spider.

Spider's this – well, the only word I can think of is "freak" – with all sorts of rings and studs sticking out of his face. Once he was in a friendly mood and he told me that he's got twenty-seven piercings – I counted twenty in his face, so that's two on his chest, one on his navel and – well, I don't like to think about the other ones. He's three years older than my sister – which my mum and dad *love* – and he makes her look like a carnivorous fascist. Honestly, he once had a go at me for wearing leather *shoes*. I pointed out that they were part of my school uniform and he said that was no excuse. To be honest, if this rebellion thing was part of a phase, I wasn't sure when my sister was likely to grow out of it.

"So what am I supposed to do?"

"Just be yourself." She was obviously trying to get rid of me.

"But I've been myself for thirteen years, and I haven't got a girlfriend."

"Maybe you haven't met the right girl."

"Who says there's a right girl? Maybe she doesn't go to my school. And anyway, how am I supposed to know when I meet her?"

"You'll just know."

"*How?*" To be honest, that came out as more of a whine than I'd expected — but it seemed to do the trick. Becky put her book down and gave me a sympathetic look. Well, sort of sympathetic.

"Dylan, I don't know what the girls in your class are like, but I didn't go for Spider because he's rebellious, or because he's an idiot. I was friends with him for ages first. There must be *some* girls in your class who like you."

"Erm. . ."

"I mean, *I* don't like you, but that's because you're my brother and you're always getting on my nerves. I'm sure the girls in your class think you're lovely."

"Um . . . thanks."

"No problem. Now get out of my room."

I shut the door on my way out. So that was how my sister found Spider. I'd always thought she used a magnet.

Let's Get This Party Started

Of course, it didn't matter if I *was* lovely – it didn't exactly help my self-confidence. When I woke up on Saturday, for instance, my first thought was "Brilliant!" Shortly followed by "Aaargh!" A tiny bit of my brain was going, *This is it. This could be the day you get together with Kate* – which was brilliant. Unfortunately, a much bigger bit was going, *What if something goes wrong? What if you spill something down yourself again? What if you can't think of anything to say? What if SHE DOESN'T LIKE YOU?* Which was . . . well, aaargh. That carried on through most of the morning and actually got worse in the afternoon, so by the evening I was practically a nervous wreck. Still, at least getting dressed wasn't much of a problem.

The thing is, I don't really have any shirts that don't look like school shirts, so the obvious choice – well, the only choice – was a T-shirt and jeans. The problems started when I got out of the shower. I noticed my sister's deodorant on the bathroom shelf – one of those ones they advertise in glossy mags and "arty" adverts – looking much cooler than your typical squirt of Lynx. Non-animal tested and non-harmful to the ozone layer, natch. It was also *supposed* to be unisex, which was why I didn't really notice until I'd experimentally sprayed it all over myself that I smelled . . . well, not quite right. I thought about having another shower, but I didn't really have time. In the end, I decided to try to cover it up with a quick dash of Lynx. Then it was time to ring Dec.

"You got the stuff?" I whispered down the phone. Dec had appointed himself in charge of The Plan, but even though he was sure he'd be able to get what we needed, I didn't want to lug my huge rucksack over to his house for no reason.

"Yeah. I talked to some mates of mine," Dec mumbled back.

"How much did you get?"

"Loads. It's going to be great." Dec hung up.

"What stuff?" asked my mum from behind me. I just about managed to avoid going "Aah!" That's always a dead giveaway.

"Stuff?" I said, innocently.

"What's Dec getting?"

Ah.

"Erm. . ." Come on, brain. "Pringles!" I said, with probably too much of an "ah-hah! *That'll* do!" tone to my voice. "Doritos. Party poppers. Paper cups. You know, party stuff."

"I see," my mum said, in her teacher voice. "You know that I don't want you getting up to anything at this party, don't you, Dylan?"

"Like what?"

"Like *anything*."

"Oh. No, there isn't going to be anything like that. It's not that kind of party."

My mum didn't look convinced, but she left it at that. I sort of wanted to tell her there was nothing to worry about – especially since the incident with Banksy's purple goop put me off beer (or whatever) for life – but I thought that if she worked out what was really going on, she'd be even more worried – because, in a way, what we were up to was even worse.

"Actually," my mum carried on. "You *smell* really nice."

"Thanks. Well, I'm going now. See you later," I said, trying to sound casual as I slung my bag over my shoulder and headed for the door.

"You look *smart* as well." My mum looked like she was trying not to laugh. "Have you actually *ironed* those jeans?"

"Yeah. I'm off to Dec's."

"Smelling like that?"

"Yes."

"Are there going to be *girls* at this party?"

Aaargh. Ever since the "incident" at the wedding – of *course* I'd had to tell her what happened – my mum'd been treating me like her little baby, ruffling my hair and saying things like "he's all grown up". She said "girls" like you'd say "Are there going to be *bears* there?" – she seemed that worried about me. I wondered if Lennon and Becky had got this treatment.

"Maybe." I tried to look like I wasn't bothered one way or the other. "I don't know. Look, I've got to run for the bus. . ."

"OK." Phew. I headed for the door. "D'you want a kiss for good luck?"

Aargh.

On the way to Dec's, I couldn't help but feel like everyone on the bus was staring at me. I suppose I deserved it, really – I smelled like a girl. I couldn't help feeling that I was trying too hard, it was really obvious and Dec and Will were going to laugh at me.

I shouldn't have worried.

By the time I arrived at his house, Dec already had his hair gelled up into deliberately scruffy spikes. He was wearing a black hoodie saying "Skateboarding Is Not A Crime" in big prison-block lettering, the baggiest trousers I've ever seen on a non-clown and – nice touch – one of those hip-chain things that you normally see attached to German Shepherd dogs. He was obviously going for the "I haven't made any effort" look. It must have taken him *ages*.

Will looked . . . different.

For a start, he was wearing a stripy shirt. He'd obviously had a go at ironing as well, but shirts are a bit trickier than T-shirts – both his sleeves and most of his collar looked like he'd just woken up from sleeping in a box. Better yet, he'd actually had a haircut, which seemed to have just about got the usual mess under control.

He actually looked pretty smart. Apart from the lightsaber.

"I forgot to tell everyone else to bring their own weapons," said Dec, giving Will a dismissive look. "D'you think they'll remember?"

Will mumbled something and stashed it in a corner.

"What's that flowery smell?" he said, walking past me.

"Dunno."

I dumped myself down in a chair. Now we just had to get everything organized. . .

Time to Party?

Dec's house is right on the outskirts of town. It isn't as big as Matt's, but the way it's laid out — tiny kitchen, massive living room, big garden — made it look like a pretty good venue for a party. The furniture was helpful, too — normally I can hardly even look at Dec's mum's taste in DFS sofas, but for a party, I reckoned, the horrendous floral patterns were perfect for hiding rogue splatters of salsa dip. We'd all brought rucksacks full of Pringles, Mini Cheddars and cherry Coke, and Will had even come up with some sour cream and guacamole that he'd found lying about his mum's fridge. I was just glad I wasn't going to be there when she noticed they were gone — she already thinks I'm a bad influence. We'd hidden everything we thought was breakable or really easily stainable, locked Dec's dad's booze cabinet and hidden the remote controls for all the stereos. We'd even chucked big plastic tablecloths over most of the easily-scuffed furniture. The goldfish in Dec's mum's horrible ornamental pond, unfortunately, were just going to have to take their chances.

By six o'clock, everything was ready. We'd told everyone the party was starting at seven, but we reckoned that everybody'd be fashionably late by arriving at about half past. At the latest, we decided, everyone should have arrived by eight.

By quarter to eight, no one had turned up. Will, looking agitated, kept picking up his lightsaber and putting it down again. Dec was pointedly messing about with his CDs, as if he'd totally expected things to turn out like this.

By eight o'clock – no one. Dec and Will were doing the yeah-we're-totally-not-bothered thing by playing fighting games on the PlayStation 2. If there's an upside to Will's complete lack of social skills, it's that he's absolutely brilliant at Tekken 4. Shame more girls aren't impressed by that sort of thing. I would've probably been worrying more about whether Kate was going to turn up ("Might see you there"? What did that mean?) but it was difficult to concentrate while they were shouting at each other.

"That doesn't count." Dec chucked down his pad in disgust. "You were just hammering the buttons."

"Yeah, and you lost." Will looked pleased that he'd finally found something he was better at than Dec. Well, something Dec cared about, anyway. "I must've been hammering the right ones, hmmm?"

"I wish you were dead. Best of three?"

"Actually, I've already beaten you twice. Best of five?" Will said, innocently.

"Fine."

By ten past eight – no one. Will and Dec had moved on to football, mainly to stop Dec from getting even more angry.

"Did you actually remember to invite *anyone*?" Will was asking, still buzzing from his fighting mastery. "Ref! Ref, that's the most obvious foul I've ever seen!"

"Yes, thanks, loads of people. Who did you ask?" Dec seemed to be getting angrier. "And it's a man's game, Will. That was a dive."

Will went red.

"There's a girl coming to meet me, actually."

"Oh, really?" Dec said, twisting his player round a defender. "What does she look like?"

Ouch. Suddenly, I regretted mentioning Mangagirl to Dec.

"Erm, she's pretty nice, you know. . ." said Will, "Oh, come on Ferdinand, what're you. . ."

"Gooooal!" shouted Dec. "Look at this. . . Look at this replay, Dylan! Left-footer from Van Nistelrooy! Genius. Well —" he turned to Will — "I can't wait to meet her."

By twenty past eight – no one.

"What're we going to do with all these crisps?" asked Will, looking around.

"I don't know, have them for breakfast, or something."

"Why d'you think nobody turned up?" asked Will, innocently.

"I don't know," muttered Dec.

"What're we going to do about The Plan?" I wondered out loud.

"I don't know!" Dec suddenly shouted. "I've put all the effort into this party! I invited everyone, I got all the stuff together, it's *my* house, and nobody's—"

Then, suddenly, the doorbell rang.

Somehow, by about quarter to nine, the living room was nearly full. Dec's mates were the first to turn up, along with a load of other lads that I only vaguely knew. They'd soon staked out all the good seats and flicked through Dec's CD collection, and were happily munching away on party snacks. Hannah and Rachel came soon afterwards, dragging all their mates with them and air-kissing Dec on the way in. Even a couple of Will's weird mates turned up – for a minute, it actually looked like they were thinking about trying to squeeze up on the sofas next to the girls, before they gave up and sat in a corner. I reckoned Dec must have invited them.

Everything seemed to be going pretty well. People were eating the crisps, talking to each other, silently playing computer games (Will's mates) and bobbing their heads in time with the music. Nobody was actually *dancing*, of course, but I reckoned that was just a matter of time. If it carried on at this rate, everything was going to be brilliant, apart from one thing – Kate obviously wasn't coming. Still, it wasn't all bad – maybe I could talk to Hannah. I was just thinking about what to say to her when I saw the skaters.

"Erm, mate, what're *they* doing here?" I said, nodding in their direction. I'd skidded up to Dec, who was busily chatting to a sympathetic-looking Rachel. He gave me a sort of nervous look, and dragged me into a corner.

"I invited them."

"But, um, do you think that's a good idea?"

"Look, mate – sorry, but Natalie's my. . ." He suddenly dropped into a whisper, "*Natalie's my girlfriend* . . . well, sort of . . . and I couldn't exactly invite *her* without letting her mates come along, could I? Besides which, who d'you think bought us the stuff for The Plan?"

I didn't answer. I was staring at Natalie. And Fiona. And the half-dozen other skater lads they'd brought along with them, all swigging out of tins that *weren't* from our pile and laughing loud enough to make the whole room turn around to look. Obviously *they'd* found something to do before eight o'clock – something like chugging blackberry-flavoured mystery juice. Dec just shrugged. Natalie waved and smirked. Then Fiona spotted me, and half-strolled, half-staggered over.

"Dylan! How are youuu? Having fun?"

She broke down into snorty giggles, puffing hot little clouds of apple-scented breath into my face. Oh, great. Fiona seemed to have forgotten about us not speaking to each other again. Pity.

"Hey, mate," said Endo, shoving past me to get at the Pringles and belching. Brilliant.

Dec was next to me, shuffling his feet. "Sorry, but you know. . ."

"Yeah, but. . ." The doorbell went, which was handy, because I had no idea what I was going to say next. I feigned a *lucky-escape-for-you* face: "Oh, hang on, I'll get that."

I stomped off to answer the door. To be honest, I was glad to get away from Dec without starting an argument. It *was* his house, and she *was* his girlfriend, and I *was* in the wrong, but . . . gah. How was I supposed to avoid a really drunk Fiona for the rest of the evening? Anyway, I was saying bad words under my breath as I opened the door.

And then, for just a moment, it didn't seem to matter that much.

"Hi."

"Hi. Erm, come in."

In physics – we did this the other day – there's a unit of time called a nanosecond. It's about the same as a millionth of a normal second, and it only really matters when you're talking about things moving at light speed or the vibrations of an atom. That, I reckon, was about how long I was happy for as Kate squeezed past me.

Then I saw who was standing directly behind her.

Going Out with a Bang

"No one invited *you*," I said to Matt, feeling less confident than I (hopefully) sounded. It didn't help that Keith was standing directly behind him. Or that I couldn't help wondering if somebody actually *had* invited him. Somebody like . . . Kate? They'd turned up together, hadn't they? So the next thing Matt said made me feel a bit better – just not much.

"Actually, Will did."

Coincidentally, at that point, Will himself skidded past, chasing after someone with a lightsaber – I was surprised that he hadn't taken out any of the furniture yet. I grabbed him.

"Will, you didn't invite Matt and Keith, did you?"

"No . . . what're you on about?"

"Work it out, Jedi boy. Use the force," said Matt, shoving past Will and stuffing a bit of paper in his hand. It didn't look like one of Dec's party invitation flyers – more like a computer printout. Will read it and – practically in slow motion – curled over. It was almost as if Matt'd thumped him. As he crumpled it up Matt grabbed a bag of Doritos and headed for the stereo.

"Thanks for inviting us, Darth," waved Keith, following him. I still didn't have a clue what was going on, but Will looked completely crushed. I'm never too good in that sort of situation.

"Losers, eh?" I tried, with a sort of eye-rolling, what-can-you-do? look. Will looked at me for a second, then dashed off. From there, everything went a bit downhill.

Look, I'm not one of those people who get really protective of their stuff. My dad, for instance, gets upset if you prop a book open (it breaks the spine), hates it when you leave CDs lying about (they get dusty) and goes absolutely *mental* if you leave a cup of tea balanced near anything electrical ("What are you trying to do, burn the house down?"). I'm not that bad. But if you're going to just turn up at a party, I don't think it's very polite to, say, immediately announce that the music's "rubbish", eject the CD, chuck it on the floor and stick your own music on. Especially if that "music" happens to be a rapper yelling about shooting "pheasant pluckers" over the sound of police sirens. As for ramping the volume up to "ear-bleeding" and ignoring everyone's polite requests to turn it down a bit, well, that's just rude. Then the shouting started.

I'd heard the banging on the wall, obviously. Matt, cleverly, had dealt with it by turning up the stereo even more, going from "floor-shaking" to "possibly life-threatening". Before long, the people in the living room looked like they could hardly think. When the thumping on the door and shouting started, you could only just hear it.

"Turn that bloody rubbish off!" yelled the red-faced man in the doorway, who'd obviously had plenty of time to work himself up into a state.

"No problem, Mr Evans. Sorry. I'll sort it out."

Dec, who'd answered the door, did his best to look apologetic.

"Not that it's any of your business," pointed out Natalie, suddenly appearing behind Dec.

"Erm, I think someone was looking for you in the kitchen, Natalie. . ." Dec mumbled, shoving her away from the front door.

"Hey, don't push. . . I was just. . . Oh, *fine*," Natalie slurred, eventually giving up and huffing off.

"Look, I think I've got a right to. . ." started Mr Evans, obviously thinking that everyone was getting off the subject.

"Calm down, grandad!" shouted Matt from the living room.

"Rest in peace, ****** ******!" yelled the rapper on the stereo.

"What the hell do you think you're playing at? Do your parents know what you're up to?" yelled Mr Evans over the racket. He wasn't going to let this go.

"It's just a few friends I've got round. I'll get them to turn it down." Dec was trying to get the door closed, without much success.

"Tell him to **** ***!" suggested Matt.

"I'll **** your *** up, ****** ******!"

added the angry rapper. This wasn't helping.

"You little ****!" It seemed Mr Evans was joining in. "I've a good mind to phone the bloody police!"

"I'll **** any ****** that ****s with my—" started the potty-mouthed rapper. Then the stereo switched itself off.

Silence.

Well, not really. Mr Evans was still threatening Dec, Dec was trying to reason with him, the skaters were still whooping and Matt and Keith were swearing at the stereo – but after the head-rattling rap madness that had just stopped, it was almost eerily quiet.

"Sorry, Mr Evans. We'll keep it down. And I'm sorry about him," said Dec gesturing at Matt and taking advantage of the momentary confusion. "If it starts getting too loud again, just let us know, OK?"

"Well, that's—" started Mr Evans, but by that time, Dec had managed to shut the door. Phew. Matt was looking around suspiciously, so I put the remote control for the stereo back in my pocket. I thought I'd probably need it again. And there was still The Plan to worry about. . .

Twenty minutes later, I was beginning to have second thoughts about parties – they just seemed too much like hard work. What with keeping an eye on the stereo, worrying about whether the skaters were going to start breaking things, and stressing about Fiona, I'd hardly had chance to talk to anyone I actually *liked*. The thrashers had stolen most of the food, but at least they'd brought their own drinks – they were even offering them around, although none of the girls from my class seemed to be interested in drinking purplish liquid from an old Fanta bottle. Especially if it was being offered to them by someone with black dread-locks and a T-shirt saying "Baby Killer". Kate was sitting watching Rachel dab her eyes with a hanky – something to do with Matt, probably – and I didn't even like to think about what was going on. Were they *talking* about Matt? I really hoped I hadn't helped his chances. Meanwhile, Dec seemed to have disappeared, Natalie seemed to have given up on looking for him, and Will was just sitting on the sofa on his own.

I wandered over and sat myself down on what could've been a decorative leaf or a splash of guacamole.

"All right?" Well, no, obviously he wasn't – but what was I supposed to say?

"Not really."

"What's up?"

Will just stared at me for a second. Then he pulled a bit of paper – Matt's bit of paper – out of his pocket and passed it to me. I unfolded it. And right in the middle:

QUIGONJINN
Fancy coming 2 a party on Saturday nite?

MANGAGIRL
Give me the address and I'll C U there! ;)

Oh dear. How could Will not fall for that? It had smileys, and everything. I never even realized Matt could work a computer.

"Ah, well," I said, trying to be breezy about it, "it's not the end of the world, is it?"

Will ignored me.

"You're probably better off meeting girls in the real world, anyway."

Silence.

"You'll meet the right, um. . ." Hang on, that wasn't the right thing to say. "Just be. . ." No, I had a feeling that "be yourself" wasn't very good advice to give someone clutching a lightsaber. "Um. . ."

I was out of things to say, but at that point Fiona thoughtfully decided to break up the tension by sprinting past, falling over my legs and landing on Will.

"Are you all right?" Will asked, suddenly looking more worried than depressed – it wasn't much of an improvement.

Fiona did her eye-widening thing and nodded a lot, casually using his leg to lever herself upright. Will managed to only look *slightly* terrified.

"Fiiiine. Who are you?" she said. Amazingly, she seemed even more spaced out than when she'd turned up. "I like your hair. . ."

"I'm. . ." started Will, but Fiona just mumbled something and slumped over on top of him, pinning him to the sofa. Will gave me a pleading look.

"You're on your own," I said. "Try poking her, or something."

Then, suddenly, a huge whistling CRACK came from outside.

"Boys and girls!" shouted Dec. "I am about to start blowing things up in the garden."

The Plan: or, How to Burn Off Your Own Eyebrows

Disclaimer: In the unlikely event that the person reading this bit thinks any of it's a Good Idea, I should point out that the procedure outlined here is not medically or scientifically advisable. I'm not seriously suggesting you try it, because IT IS NOT A GOOD IDEA and if you do, I take no responsibility. Fair enough? Let's do some science. . .

Part 1: Equipment
  You will need:
– A back garden with a big patio, and someone stupid enough to let you use it.
– A friction-powered Jokermobile (with Real Turbo Action).

– A Batman toy (Hang-Gliding Action optional).
– A Game of Life (or other unwanted board game).
– A variety of explosives (read, fireworks – your local friendly gang of hardcore skaters might buy you a box).
– Lots of other flammable stuff.
  And, most importantly:
– A fire extinguisher.

Part 2: Preparations

Ever seen the TV series of *Batman*? Not the cartoon – I'm talking about the campy sixties version where Adam West wore grey tights and you could see The Joker's moustache under his make-up. Lennon watches it all the time, because he says it's cleverly retro, rather than just rubbish. Well, anyway, every episode came in two parts, and at the end of the first part, The Joker always tied Batman to something – a big pendulum, or a conveyor belt in an evil ice-cream factory, or something – and then wandered off, leaving Batman with only a utility belt full of incredibly high-tech gadgets to defend himself. This, obviously, was a stupid plan. Ours was much better.

Basically, this was the idea: Ninja Action Batman (with Hang-Glider!) was going to be the centre-piece of an explosive masterpiece, set off by the evil Jokermobile (with Real Turbo Action!). With a Game of Life board as a base that Will claimed to have never actually played (who actually wants to pretend they've got a baby and a mortgage? weird), we superglued Batman down, stuck a load of bangers to his costume, and surrounded him with fireworks. Then we stuck some sparklers to the front of the Jokermobile as "ignition devices". Then, just in case the friction wheels weren't enough to propel it the eight or so metres we thought counted as a "safe distance", we put a couple of rockets on the back. Then we covered Batman in hairspray. Whatever was in Batman's utility belt, he was probably going to be stuffed.

Quick explosive tip: If you're planning on using hairspray in an experiment, don't let the actual can anywhere near the display unless you're fairly sure you don't want your face any more. What you're already doing is dangerous enough, and throwing what's basically a big shrapnel-bomb into the mix is so stupid I'm not even sure there's a word for it.

Part 3: Results and Conclusions

Instead of everyone dashing outside, it took Dec about ten minutes to round up all the mashed skaters and girls who'd forgotten to bring proper jackets with them – not planning on standing around in the garden, probably. Will managed to prise Fiona off his knees – we thought about putting her in the recovery position or something, realized neither of us knew it, and opted for the dribbling-on-the-sofa position instead, which seemed to work fine. By that time, everyone else was standing outside shivering, including Kate, so we dashed out to watch as Dec lit the fuse.

At that point, things stopped going according to plan.

Looking back, I think the main problem was that instead of making a "controlled" approach towards the main firework dump, the Jokermobile refused to budge at all – until the rocket engines went off. At that point, it jumped forward, ricocheted off a wonky patio stone, flipped over and exploded right in the middle of the pile of fireworks. Straight after that, everything else on the pile seemed to go up in one huge blast. Ever seen what an exploding Batman figure looks like? Neither have I – because by the time that happened, everyone was already ducking for cover and screaming.

To the Batmobile!

When the skaters started whooping and high-fiving each other, I decided it was probably safe to stop protecting my eyes with my arm. Then I wished I'd run for it as well. Kate had disappeared, Will was still looking glum, and most of the It girls had run back inside. Chris and a few other lads were still shuffling nervously around, but Dec was the first person to actually speak.

"Hmm. That wasn't quite what I was expecting."

"That was cool!" yelled a skater.

"I'm going home!" announced one of the It girls, struggling into her coat. "That was the stupidest thing I've ever seen."

"Cheers," said Dec, still looking a bit fazed.

"Bye!" yelled another skater. "Are there any more fireworks about?"

"No," lied Dec.

Five minutes later, the wreckage was still burning. It was quite soothing to watch, really, except for when the flames occasionally caught an unexploded firework and set it off with a massive bang. There didn't seem to be much point in using the fire extinguisher, because the whole mess was safely on the paving slabs and seemed unlikely to start raging out of control – but nobody wanted to try stamping on it, just in case a roman candle suddenly melted their trainers.

"We could toast marshmallows," someone suggested.

"Hmm. I think there's still quite a lot of hairspray on there," Dec pointed out. I thought he'd left it a bit late to be safety conscious.

"There can't be much left to burn, can there?" somebody else said.

"Haven't got a clue," said Dec. "I thought everything flammable went up in the first blast."

"Is it still dangerous?" asked one of Will's mates. Dec looked at him.

"Yes. Yes, Zeppo, I think the big pile of burning fireworks is still probably a bit dangerous."

"What the *hell* are you playing at now?" interrupted Mr Evans, from over the fence. *Uh-oh.*

"Just some fireworks, Mr Evans," tried Dec. "Nothing to worry about."

"Do your parents know what you're up to? Because I'm going to have a pretty stern—"

"Blaaaargh," interrupted someone from inside. We all looked around, and then immediately wished we hadn't. Fiona had woken up – and it looked as if she'd been picking up bad habits from her mum. Although she hadn't even bothered with trying to make it to a nearby toilet cubicle.

"Bleuuurgh."

Dec just stared at her for a couple of seconds. Then he turned to a horrified Will.

"Get a bucket out from under the sink will you, mate?"

With Will holding a hastily grabbed saucepan under Fiona's mouth and Dec trying to steer her towards the bathroom, I suddenly didn't have much to do. The living room was still packed full of skaters, but they'd taken over even more of the floor – most of the It girls had apparently run home when the exploding and shouting started. Even Natalie seemed to have disappeared — probably because Dec was looking more worried about his mum's carpets than her. I'd have liked to help scrape up the mess Fiona had left behind, but, well, I don't know what gets puke out of carpet, and I didn't really want to. Besides, she wasn't *technically* my girlfriend, so it wasn't my problem.

Then, out of nowhere, I noticed Kate sitting on the steps. She seemed pretty much immune to the skaters. She didn't even mind the occasional flash from the Game of . . . um, Melting Batman. And I hadn't even had a chance to talk to her.

This is it! my brain was shouting. *This is what you're here for! Try not to embarrass me, eh?*

I sat down next to her as casually as I could. Which wasn't very casually.

"Enjoying the party?"

She looked at me. Then she glanced around at a random skater swigging cider out of a two litre bottle, the Idiots playing sparkler duels and the wreckage of the Bat-firework.

"Yeah! It's been . . . interesting."

We both had a little smirk at that. *Hahaha,*

went my brain, *now think of something clever to say.*

"D'you, um, fancy a dance?"

Oh, nice one, went my brain, sarcastically. Kate gave me a confused look.

"Do *you*?"

I looked at the only people dancing – skaters moshing along to thrash-rock – and couldn't help smiling a bit.

"No, not really."

"No, me neither." Kate started giggling. "I really, really don't."

We both turned around to look at the skaters properly, and I started giggling too.

"What are they *doing*?"

Kate was sniggering uncontrollably, now.

"They're rubbish!"

"And mental."

"Look at that one!"

"He's going to give himself whiplash!"

Pretty soon, we were both just staring at the mad hair-throwing going on and laughing out loud. By the time two Korn fans accidentally headbutted each other, I'd nearly given myself a stitch.

Now! my brain was shouting. *This is it! Come onnn!*

"So. . ." I started, trying to think of something – *anything* – to say next. "Soooo . . . erm, did you come with Matt?"

Oh, genius, went my brain. *I'll just leave you to it, shall I?*

"No. . ." Kate looked puzzled. "He just sort of followed me up the road with that mate of his. Why?" She smiled. "Are you here with anyone?"

Erk. Something in my brain flipped on a warning siren – but just as I was trying to think of a cool (and sort-of-truthful, in case she'd been talking to the skaters) answer – Fiona dashed past us and started puking into the pond. Will, who'd been following her with a bucket, stood behind her and helped hold her hair back – although that wasn't exactly going to help out any goldfish that got in the way. I turned back to Kate.

"No. Well, not really."

"That's a shame."

"Hmm."

We both went quiet for a bit. Maybe Kate was thinking about what a beautiful night it was, or how nice the smouldering plastic looked in the moonlight, or something tranquil. My brain, on the other hand, was working at top speed trying to think of something witty/clever/romantic to say. It's terrible at that sort of thing.

Finally, I managed:

"D'you think maybe we could—"

"Ten points for a garden gnome!"

BANG.

All right. So that wasn't Kate.

BANG.

"Nearly got that one!"

It was Matt and Keith.

BANG.

In all the chaos and mess, we'd all forgotten the golden rule of dealing with fireworks: Keep Out of Reach of Idiots. And now the Idiots were throwing bangers at little defenceless garden ornaments. Typical, eh?

BANG.

"Ye-es! He shoots, he scores!"

Dec annoys me sometimes. He's occasionally got some stupid ideas about girls, he's a bit thoughtless, and he's got *awful* taste in music — but he's my mate. And when your mate throws a party, you can't just stand by and let Idiots throw bangers at his patio decorations. Even when you're *incredibly* close to thinking of a brilliant line that's really going to impress the girl sitting next to you — which, honestly, I'm sure I was. But the goldfish were having enough trouble without a stray firework landing in the pond. So I did the only thing I could.

"Sorry, Kate — hold on just a second?"

I armed myself with the only thing to hand, and marched over to confront the rocketeers.

Matt and Keith were just trying to get another banger going, giggling. I stood there, trying to be calm, with my hands behind my back — my secret weapon was probably going to rely on the element of surprise. If I'd been James Bond, I'm sure I'd have come up with a great line at this point. Something like:

"Party's over, boys. Haven't you read the fireworks code?"

Or, even better:

"Sorry, chaps — I'm supposed to be keeping the dumb animals away from the explosives."

Instead, I managed to come up with:

"Pack that in."

"You what?" Matt totally ignored me. Keith turned around, looking more surprised than annoyed.

"Erm, I said, pack it in," I said again, raising my voice a bit. "I don't go round to your house and chuck bangers at your golden retrievers, do I?"

Matt stopped, looking genuinely shocked for a second. Then he did his evil smile.

"We've still got loads of those sparklers left, haven't we, Keith?"

"Yeah. Shall we grab him?"

"Let's grab him." Matt started walking towards me.

To be honest, I wasn't sure what the connection was between "loads of sparklers" and "grabbing me", but I was fairly certain it wasn't going to be anything good. Ever seen – or experienced – that thing where you pick someone up by their arms and legs and slam them into a bike-shed pole, spuds-first? It's not too pleasant. Well, that's Matt's idea of a productive breaktime – he's pretty big on "hurting you" first and "thinking about the consequences" later.

So when Matt said, "Get his legs," I brought the fire extinguisher out from behind my back and let them have it.

Pffffrt.

I don't know whether you've ever shot someone with a fire extinguisher, but I don't recommend it. For a start, it ruins their clothes –

Matt and Keith looked like they'd been hit by a giant exploding marshmallow. Secondly, it doesn't slow them down for very long, but it makes them really, really angry. Even if they're an Idiot and they really deserve it – well, just bear in mind that you've only got about five seconds to dish out the foam justice before you run out of ammo and they decide to kick your head in.

Fortunately, it was about that point that the police turned up.

The Morning After

"So your mum and dad were all right about everything?"

Dec stirred his coffee. It was Sunday afternoon, so I reckoned that even the fact that he'd managed to meet me in the cafe – i.e. that he wasn't indefinitely grounded – was probably a good sign. Then again, he might have just run for it first thing in the morning, and been staring mournfully at his grande latte all day.

"Well, no, not really. They shouted quite a lot, but it could've been worse. At least I managed to get rid of all the melted plastic."

It had looked pretty bad for a while, to be honest. When the police arrived, Matt and Keith couldn't kill me any more – always helpful – but I reckoned my mum and dad'd do it for them if

I ended up getting driven home in a squad car. Fortunately, Will's mates had sprung into action – none of them like the Idiots – and reassured everyone that I'd been acting purely out of self defence. Mr Evans – who'd snitched on us – came round to offer helpful advice along the lines of "Lock them all up", so the police sent most people home and gave Dec a verbal warning just to keep Mr Evans quiet. Will, me, Fiona and another couple of sleeping, worse for wear skaters stayed, but the party was over. Between me and Dec, we managed to get most of the fish into some of his mum's mixing bowls, where they were all right for long enough for the pond filter to get rid of most of the half-digested White Lightning. After that, I didn't want to just leave Dec to face his parents alone, but . . . well, actually that's a lie. I really did. So even though I was supposed to be staying for the night, I'd had to make the phone call I was dreading.

"Hello?"

"*Becky?*" Thank – well, whoever – for hippies. My sister was still up at midnight – probably planning her next protest march – and for once, she had a proper excuse to use the car. Not that

that stopped her from having a go at me as soon as she turned up.

"What've you been *doing*?" she said, sniffing the air. There was still a fairly strong whiff of gunpowder floating around. And my trousers had quite a few foam/grass/salsa dip stains on them. Still, as long as my mum didn't see them, I thought I'd be OK.

"Gatecrashers." I shrugged. "You know what it's like."

"So is she your girlfriend?" Becky asked, looking in Fiona's direction.

I hadn't even had another chance to talk to Kate before her mum arrived. She'd waved goodbye as she rushed out the door – around the time the police turned up. *Damn* – I might have saved a few of Dec's mum's goldfish from a messy end but I'd completely blown my big chance with her. I was about to answer Becky when Dec glanced at Fiona, still sitting on the sofa and looking queasy and said, "Yeah, maybe you could give your girlfriend a lift."

Fiona did a miniature burp, then looked suspiciously like she was swallowing something. I turned back to Becky.

"He's trying to be funny. I'm still waiting for the right girl."

Becky gave a little snort in my direction. Still, she'd managed to turn up before we could start scraping all the charred plastic off the patio, and I hadn't even had to spend half an hour explaining why I wasn't spending the night at Dec's to my mum. I was so relieved, I've decided never to mock Becky's hippy hypocrisy again. Maybe.

"So, would you call that a successful party?" I asked Dec, twirling my coffee around.

"In my experience, no."

"Everyone'll be talking about it for ages."

"Yeah, including my mum and dad." Dec dumped some more chocolate in his mocha. "Anyway, how did it go with Kate? I saw you talking to her."

"Dunno. I said *something*, but . . . oh, you know." I shrugged. "I'll see her around. Sorry if I let the side down."

"Well, you weren't the only one." Dec stirred his coffee furiously. "I split up with Natalie."

"What happened?"

"Oh, I don't know. She said she'd snogged

somebody else last week. Probably some skater prat."

"Really?"

"And, um. . ." Dec frowned. "To be honest, I'd sort of already asked Rachel out by the time she told me. So I'm not really that bothered." Typical.

"What did Rachel say?"

"Well, I think she's probably going to get back with Matt. . . But I'll find someone else."

"Don't go setting me up with any more thrashers, though, eh?" I said, only a little bit upset that Rachel hadn't been there to see Matt threatening to stuff fireworks down my trousers.

"Fair enough. I'll find somebody else to be my wingman next time."

We both had a contemplative slurp of mochaccino.

"What happened to Fiona?" I said, breaking the thoughtful pause.

"Erm, I think she ended up snogging someone else. Sorry, mate."

"Don't worry about it. Essence of carrot-chunks doesn't do much for me."

"Oh, so now you're getting *picky*. Hey, look everyone – Dylan's all grown up."

"Shut up. I . . . hang on, who did she snog?"

It was just then that Will walked in. Whistling. Well, trying to whistle.

"Enjoy last night, chaps?" If this was Will trying to be cool, it wasn't working very well.

"Not really," Dec said, not taking the bait. "I nearly got arrested, then I spent half an hour picking bits of Dorito out of a fishpond. I think it's fair to say it didn't go exactly as I planned."

"I made some lifelong enemies," I said, thinking about Matt. "That's always nice."

"Oh, really? That's a pity." Will gave us a little sheepish grin. "I quite enjoyed it."

I'm fairly sure this was supposed to come out as "casual", but it ended up as "desperate-for-attention". I didn't want to ask — but one of us had to.

"So, um, what did you get up to?"

"Oh, y'know, I met this girl. We don't have a lot in common, but she seemed really nice."

"Are you going to see her again?"

"Yeah, I think so. She was feeling a bit ill, but she was pretty keen."

Dec and I just looked at each other.

"Probably just a bit of food poisoning," said Dec.

"Definitely." I nodded. "Something in the guacamole, I expect. Or maybe it runs in the family."

"Hmm. . ." said Will, suddenly getting suspicious.

"Well, good luck, mate."

"Yeah. Get yourself a latte to go," said Dec, with a generous wave. "Tell them to put it on my tab."

After a bit of a disagreement when it turned out that Dec didn't have a tab – or, in fact, any money – we wandered off into the Sunday shopping crowd. Just as we were leaving the cafe, I saw the waitress – the one who always scowled.

I was in such a good mood that I smiled at her without even thinking about it. And she . . . smiled . . . back.

Sigh.

Just got this e-mail:

Hello Dylan!
I accept your kind offer! Maybe we will play cricket and see Big Ben! I look forward to your tea and cakes! Please thank your mother

*and father for generously agreeing to keep
me! Until February!
Tchuss
Rudi*

He's insane. I just hope my mum knows what
she's got me into. . .

Will Dylan survive the German exchange?

Find out in:

They Think
it's all
Over

Usually, Monday mornings rank somewhere behind "Playing Rugby With The Idiots" and "Visiting My Crazy Aunt Jess" on the list of stuff I'm looking forward to. This Monday was different, though – I finally had the chance to get rid of Rudi. And I wasn't disappointed.

"I know! They can't even speak any German! *Unglaublich!*"

"Hahaha!"

Or something like that, anyway.

As the Germans paraded into our classroom, they all somehow gravitated to the same table near the back until they were the biggest, most noticeable group in the room – trying to ignore all the day-glo jackets and laughter was practically impossible. I couldn't make out a single word of the flurry of excited chatter, but I was guessing that they were talking about the same things as us, or basically:

1. How weird their exchange partners were,

2. What a strange weekend they'd had, and. . .

3. How terrible we were at speaking their language.

OK, so we weren't talking about that last one.

"And have you seen all the pigeons? *Mein Gott!*"

"Hahaha!"

I'd huddled together with Will and Chris to compare notes on our penfriends. Chris's penfriend, Jochen, who I'd last seen getting shot to bits by Will shortly before we got chucked out of Laser Quest, was incredibly quiet. Apparently he'd shut himself in his room as soon as he got back to Chris's, hardly said a word during tea and looked incredibly relieved when he'd been allowed to phone his mum. Chris actually thought he'd heard him crying – maybe he'd forgotten his chocolate spread, or something.

Will, on the other hand, had had a great weekend. Andreas – his penfriend – had turned up with presents for all Will's family, including an illustrated history of Heidelberg, a Bach CD and a huge bag of Gummi Bears. Even better, it turned out that they were into all the same girl-frightening stuff – mainly wrestling, comics and anything involving machine guns. Apparently, Andreas had even offered to show Will how to do a wrestling-style powerbomb – I mean, to some people that'd be a threat, but to Will it was like meeting someone who'd been to the moon. He still turned the chance down, though – I don't think he was as worried about breaking his neck as he was about what his mum'd say when she saw him in the hospital.

"What's yours like, Dylan?" asked Chris, looking glum. "Has he offered to show you any wrestling moves?"

"Nope," I said, wishing I *could* chuck Rudi through a table. "He just complains about every-thing and talks about Germany all the time."

"At least he *talks*," said Chris. "Mine hardly does *anything*."

Dec had wandered over during our conversation and now he nudged me.

"What's Kate's called again?"

"Um, Marika, I think," I said, trying to sound like I hadn't really noticed Kate's shampoo-ad penfriend. As if. "Why?"

"Well. . ." Dec glanced around in a not-at-all-suspicious-honest way, "Matt keeps looking at her, that's all."

"So?" I said, starting to get a sort of sinking feeling.

"Well, what happens if Matt gets all friendly with what's-her-name, and suddenly it's all, 'Ooh, isn't he *nice*', and Kate starts talking to him and, well, you know. . ."

"I don't think Matt's *got* a nice side," I said, glancing around.

The awful thing about Matt the Idiot is, I used to actually be *friends* with him. Of course, that was ages ago – before he got his current gang of Idiot mates, before he started playing rugby, and *ages* before he grew to unstoppable size and started picking on my other mates. Of course, I couldn't be friends with him after all that – and anyway, I shot him with a fire extinguisher pretty recently, which I didn't think he'd forgiven me for. Sure enough, this particular morning he was sitting in the corner, making stupid muffled comments with his gang, but . . . well, now that I looked, he *did* keep glancing towards Marika and Kate's table. I suddenly got a rush of stupid over-protectiveness – then Kate looked over at me again and I immediately felt my face heat up like a tomato in a microwave. Fortunately, though, it didn't take long before Matt showed his true colours.

"Five–one!" (cough) "Five–one!"

Honestly. First the trains, then the weather, now this. I'd spent half the walk to school trying to convince Rudi that English football hooligans weren't anywhere near as bad as he'd heard (he seemed to think most people went to Old Trafford armed) and now I had a minor hooligan coughing abuse from the opposite end of the room. I mean, I get excited about the World Cup and every-thing, but Germany've beaten us at football loads of times. . . Even if they do dive a lot.

"Two world wars –"

I thought about telling Matt to shut up, but he was still in a bad mood with me after the fire extinguisher incident. Besides, what would he do? Go "make me", then shout even louder, probably. I decided not to risk it.

"– and one World Cup!"

"Shut up, Matt." The Idiots looked round. Rachel Thorne was sitting with her arms folded and an I'm-not-impressed frown on her face. "Stop being so stupid."

"Sor-rry." Matt gave her an I-don't-care grin and turned around.

Matt and Rachel are – usually – one of our school's "couples". If our class had its own version of *Heat*, they'd be the Posh 'n' Becks – or maybe the Jordan 'n' Peter – in every issue. The thing is, though, they keep it interesting by having these "off" phases, where they stop going out with each other for a couple of weeks. Usually when this happens, Rachel spends an entire breaktime crying, then the next few days acting as if she can't *believe* she ever went out with someone so childish. Then Matt gets Keith, or Darren, or one of his co-idiots to ask her out for him again, and they start all over again, usually with a display of rampant face-sucking on the field. It gets even more boring than the real *Heat*, honestly.

"Some of them're quite cute, anyway," I heard Hannah saying, as Rachel turned back to her table. I really hoped she wasn't talking about Rudi. My ego's pretty fragile at the best of times.

"Hmm. . ." said Rachel, looking thoughtful. "Why's that one wearing his bag on his front?"

I looked over. Sure enough, Rudi still had his rucksack firmly strapped on, as if he was expecting someone to try and steal it the second he took it off. He glanced over at me, then turned back to his friends.

"*Ich glaube germangermangerman.*"

"Hahaha!"

This was driving me mad. And it didn't stop there. . .

"*Wilkommen in England, germangermangerman,*" said Miss Spencer, and got a little laugh from the exchange students.

I couldn't really blame her for showing off — after all, she probably had a degree, or something, and most of the time she had to limit herself to conversations about ordering carrots or finding the sports centre. Besides, she's really pretty, so I tend to let her off a lot.

"OK, *Klasse.* This week, we've got a special

treat for you," she said, turning to the rest of us. "Since most of you have got guests to look after this week, it wouldn't be fair to expect you to do homework as well."

There were a few little "Yess!"-es from around the room. Miss Spencer was still smiling – but in that evil I'm-not-finished-with-you-yet way that only teachers and supervillains can do.

"So: everyone who *doesn't* have a penfriend will be doing chapter six for next Monday. . ."

There was an explosion of outrage at how unfair this apparently was. Matt, who's usually more interested in carving random shapes into his desk than taking part in lessons, seemed to think it was an injustice on the scale of being locked up for a murder you didn't commit. I thought about offering to do the work for him if he'd take Rudi home, but decided that that probably wouldn't make my mum very happy. Miss Spencer just waited patiently until everyone was reasonably quiet again.

"As I was saying, everyone who hasn't got a guest will be carrying on with book work – and everyone who *has* will be taking part in next Monday's special assembly on German culture."

This time it was the other half of the class's turn

to start shouting. How were we supposed to keep our penfriends occupied *and* work on an assembly project? What if our penfriends refused to help? How were we supposed to know anything about German culture? Miss Spencer tactfully ignored all these objections.

"It can be a famous song, a German author, anything you like – but you'd better come up with *something*," she said, giving us one of her I-might-be-pretty-but-I'm-still-mean looks. "It might be a good idea if you get your guest to help you."

I looked around at Rudi, who was sitting at the back of the classroom with his walkman on, bobbing his head up and down and mouthing lyrics to himself. *Brilliant idea*, I thought – I bet German assemblies are much better than English ones.